Things Fall Together

A Jane Luck Adventure

By Joy Outlaw

Things Fall Together: A Jane Luck Adventure

Copyright © 2017 by Joy Outlaw

OmniMind Media

Cover Graphics by
Melissa Wales

ISBN 978-0-9971827-2-9 (Print)
ISBN 978-0-9971827-3-6 (eBook)

Join the Adventure

There's more to come from the Jane Luck Adventures series and from Joy Outlaw. Stay in the know about new book releases, events, and giveaways, and join intriguing chats with the author and other readers.

Get Joy's next book and post your amazon reviews here:
amazon.com/author/joyoutlaw

Follow Joy here:
www.inanna-joy.com
Instagram   @inannajoy
Facebook   facebook.com/inanna.joy.1

Acknowledgements

Eternal Thanks,

To My Family for being my ride-or-dies.

To Nikki and Karen for being willing to put your hands to the plow and support me, and being flexible with plans that changed.

To my mentor, Dora, for every breakthrough you've pushed me to.

To Michelle Mitchell Day, Marketing Specialist; Brandon Herbin of WVCW Radio; Kimberly Ross-Hollingsworth, CEO of Arts & Authors Extravaganza; Writer and Director Jackie J. Stone; and Bertice Berry, Ph.D, Sociologist, Author, Lecturer, and Educator -- for being wellsprings of information and inspiration.

Dedication

To those who are determined to fly,

but haven't quite found their wings.

Part 1

Dreams never really die,
they haunt you like zombies instead.

1

From the gateway between life and death, she sang to me with jubilance, intrepid.

I'm runnin' for my life
I'm runnin' for my life

I was struck with wonder and couldn't believe my eyes. I'd never known my grandma Sadie to own a home so huge and grand. Yet there she was, singing and rocking away in a rocking chair between two massive, porch columns. Was this her heavenly reward, or had she come back to earth? In my cloudy dream state, I didn't know the difference.

It was a majestic, white mansion on a hill with its front double doors so tall and its porch so big and wide, it dwarfed Grandma's humble appearance. I could feel that this was all hers, and that she was proud. She wanted me to know. She stood, waved me forward, and clapped to her song.

I'm runnin' for my li-ife
I'm runnin' for my life

I could see that this house was just as she'd described. It was the one she always wanted, bigger than the homes her sons had owned after their successful years as shipyard workers and servicemen.

It was older— maybe hundreds of years older— and statelier with more character than any of those modern-day, "slap 'em up" houses her snooty neighbors' kids lived in. I just knew there were enough rooms for all of us to visit, sprawl out around her and stay for as long as we pleased, giving her welcome company.

She beamed with satisfaction, looked up at me, and took my hand with a smirk and a twinkle in her eyes.

The words to one of her favorite prayer meeting songs poured from her heart, ironic, loud and clear. Her untrained voice was throaty and smoky as ever, and every bit as sure as she was of her own victory. She swayed gently, inviting me to do the same.

If anybody asks you
what's the matter with me, me-e-e,
just tell 'em I'm saved, sanctified,
and I'm runnin' for my life

I listened and relished the sound of her voice as it slowly faded away and the sight of her and the gorgeous mansion evaporated again into darkness. It was disappointing, seeing her leave and waking up to the same old mess that surrounded me when I fell asleep. Lifting the morning's prayer would be an utter strain, but I did it anyway after several long, deep breaths.

"Lord, I am tired. I know I'm young and maybe I don't have a right to be, but I am. I'm tired of exhausting myself and failing. I'm tired of asking for permission to live, to grow, to be me. I'm tired of running. Give me a safe place to land, where I can breathe."

That was it. No pleasantries, no more groveling and attempting to shrink and appear humble. God knew what was up, supposedly. He knew what I was thinking and frankly, I figured He should be happy that I chose not give Him the raw, unfiltered version.

I rubbed my eyes and opened them, despite a voice inside me crying out that it was not ready to see the light of day. Eventually, I looked around and decided that the sight outside wasn't so bad. I'd have to face it and choose to see the good.

I pulled out of the roadside parking space. Seconds later, I was stopped in my tracks by an unnecessarily long red light. Typical.

While waiting and staring up at the clear blue sky just beyond the roof of the six-story building where my cozy, top-floor bachelorette pad used to be, I imagined the word boldly written in fluffy, white cloud font:

E V I C T E D

"That's right girl," I thought. *"they threw your ass out. Now, that's some adulthood for you."*

Well, at least it wasn't one of those pitiful all-my-junk-piled-up-on-the-curb scenes. I knew resistance would be pointless, so I just put my larger items in storage and packed the rest into my car as soon as I got word from the notice on my door. The jig was up. The relatively carefree phase of my young adulthood was officially over, and life would show the world who I really was. I wasn't a talented recent grad with a promising career. I wasn't a buppie, a rising architect. I wasn't a "catch" for some equally virtuous future gentleman. I wasn't even sure of my faith anymore.

I was depleted— mentally, physically, and spiritually. I had done all that I was told to do, and my life was still falling apart. All that I had assumed to be reality was proving to be an illusion.

"Maybe you should try a career in sales… A career… in sales." I dryly said to myself, repeating what was said to me by the principal of a small, center city architecture firm at a recent job interview.

After seeing my bright smile and spirited presentation then running his pasty fingers across the resume which highlighted my relegation to the ranks of glorified secretaries, he had concluded that sales would be a good fit for me. If my previous boss didn't trust me enough to let me do actual design work, and instead utilized the bulk of my skills in the preparation of marketing materials and filing systems, why should this guy groom me for anything better?

Marketing firms were hiring desperate graduates. I could be an "Account Manager" for one of those companies, which could always use an influx of poor, clueless, debt-laden young adults to hock random services and subscriptions door-to-door.

"At least you're a good bullshitter," is what he might as well have said.

The economy was so bad that seasoned pros were lapping up the jobs that we lower level grunts might have otherwise had access to, and they were willing to take the significant pay cuts just to stay working. Those types were much more preferable to grads like me with little design experience and barely passing grades. We newbies were shaping up to become what journalists would later refer to as the "lost generation of architects", a massive talent purge from the field. Those journalists also said that we were experiencing the highest rate of unemployment of all professions, though the American Institute of Architects never kept track of such data. Architects collectively like to maintain an image of strength.

Even if the crisis hadn't left thousands of projects stalled and firms dormant, I was convinced my brown skin and anatomy, along with my bleeding ego and plummeting confidence, all meant that I would have had a hard road to tread anyway. Maybe he was right.

Honking cars began to pile up behind me as I sat at the corner of West Johnson and Greene Streets reminiscing — about waking up on Saturday mornings and looking out the wall-to-wall picture window in my living room, about sitting on my couch sipping tea in the buff as my cares rose from the cup and evaporated into thin air, about happily allowing building management to use my apartment as a model whenever they wanted to show a prospective tenant how pleasant life in The Duval could be.

Someone behind me was pretty upset that I didn't take advantage of the two-second window of opportunity to swing out in front of oncoming traffic just before the light turned green. It was the Philly way and an opportunity that I usually took, but this time I was in a daze.

"I'm movin'. I'm movin'." I reassured them as I inched out in anticipation of a break in the oncoming cars then finally made the left turn onto Greene Street.

I must have cut it pretty close, because some random dude in a car to my left saw the need to reprimand me after I made my turn. He just pointed to the matte black, front left fender on my otherwise golden Chevy Cavalier, as if that was some indication that I was a bad driver.

"It was hit while parked on the side of the road, you moron!"

I didn't care that he couldn't hear me yelling. People never ceased to annoy me with their assumptions.

I wasn't quite sure where I'd end up. The garden style apartments immediately to the right were clad in brick with a gorgeous Tudor-style exterior and hardwood floors inside. I had scoped out a place over there, too, prior to choosing my one bedroom in the Duval. Ultimately, I couldn't resist top floor living in a building with controlled access.

Goodbye beautiful Greene Manor. Goodbye Duval.

Many times, I had considered volunteering at the nursing home directly to the left, but never fit it into my schedule. Sorry, Cliveden.

I drove a little further up the street to the Upsal Station, which I started using more frequently for trips into Center City after landing a job at the bank. I was just starting to get more comfortable with taking the train instead of the bus. The underground concourses were becoming a little less scary.

I pulled into the lot of the Point of Destination Café, just in front of the station platform, and stared down Upsal Street.

"Why not dream?" I asked myself as I drove back into the street, this time heading down Pelham Road.

To the right was another apartment complex owned by the same company that had just kicked me out of my place at The Duval. That was where I used to faithfully drop off my rent payments before my own personal downward spiral paralleled the declining economy. I picked up speed as I passed it.

I slowed down again while crossing over Horter Street and braced myself for the approach to the house that I had already made a faith claim to, the one that I dreamed of one day turning into a secret bed-and-breakfast-style retreat space for artists… or something like that, a hidden treasure in the heart of West Mount Airy.

"This is what's eating at you, Jane." I thought to myself. *"This is the reason for your wishful thinking and for yet another dream about Grandma Sadie."*

At this point, the house was totally a diamond in the rough. It was a phenomenal (and phenomenally dilapidated) Colonial-ish, Greek Revival bathed in white. The front exterior was like a smaller version of the house from the Fresh Prince of Bel Air, with a symmetrical layout and central entry lined with soaring Corinthian columns. Unlike most of the surrounding homes, it was elevated about six feet above the street— once by a three-foot grade that created the beautiful green mini plateau that the home sat on, and again by the home's three-foot stone foundation. It took two different sets of brick steps to reach it.

I had once visited this house with Jack out of pure nosiness. He had no interest in buying a house in a historic district, and it wasn't even for sale at the time. But somehow, we were able to get a peek after catching the owner smoking a little herb on the porch and feeding him some story about me doing a neighborhood case study for design class. It was sort of true.

The barely tended shrubs and vines along with the tarp that blew in the breeze, halfway covering the sunroom, gave us some indication of what we'd find inside: hardwood floors and crumbling crown molding begging for restoration; peeling, lead-based paint galore; ancient cabinetry in a kitchen which was gutted of appliances and clearly not in use; fireplaces waiting to be revived and lit.

The home's seven bedrooms all had some signs of water damage from the leaking roof. And I would definitely need to build in at least one additional bathroom in order to accommodate the quests who would eventually visit my rescued, suburban "Villa".

I wanted this house so bad it hurt. Jack told me that the owner had acquired it by way of adverse possession. Previous owners had abandoned it. Then this guy's family simply squatted on it long enough to fulfill the state's time requirement before petitioning the court for ownership.

He couldn't afford to remodel it, but, considering the current state of the housing market, he'd still make out like a bandit if he sold it at the right time. I could only dream about who would get it next and how they'd turn it into something spectacular again.

As I drove by this time, I noticed a hand-drawn "For Sale" sign out front. With Sharpie scrawled on cardboard, it was a far cry from the crisp, professional realtors' signs that peppered the historic neighborhood, but it fit this situation to a tee.

"Hope springs eternal!" I said as I made a mental note to google the address for sale information. Of course I had no money, but the availability alone was enough to keep me fantasizing. I left Pelham Road and went back to the parking lot of The Duval, just for a few minutes, to regroup and decide what to do for the night.

2

"What are you gonna do now?" I thought. I attempted to conjure up sensible Jane, my inner Receptionist, to keep me focused on solutions. *"You could move back home, but if finding work in your profession is hard here, it will probably be impossible there. And you know you love this city. Just stay put, and work your plan. Flip-flopping will only set you back."*

Philly was definitely where I wanted to be. Honestly, that was the main reason why I had no intention of moving back to Virginia. Home was just too small. I needed to be in a place where my head and heart would have plenty of space to take a deep breath, where there were plenty of options to try out so that I could eventually find something that would be the right fit for me.

"You have enough money to stay in a hotel for a couple of weeks— just enough to make it to next payday. Then you'll be

able to afford another two weeks. *If you find a place cheap enough, maybe you can put the deposit on your credit card—"*

"Nope!" I said aloud, remembering that many landlords didn't like shouldering the fees associated with credit card processing. And that didn't even matter, because I no longer had a credit card. After my bankruptcy discharge was granted, the account for the only card I had for emergencies was closed.

I decided to just stay in a hotel for as long as it took me to save up for a new place. In the meantime, I'd tap some contacts from Jack's old real estate investor list and try to find a really cheap place that wasn't totally run down. I'd have to focus on the outskirts of his contacts list though, in order to avoid anyone too close to him who may be able to trace me back to his death.

For a moment, I considered how Jack may have come to my rescue if he was still here and found me in this situation. I knew that he would never have allowed me to even get to this point. He certainly wouldn't have me scraping the bottom of the available rental barrel for something under $650 per month.

"Are you kidding me?" My inner Receptionist asked, snapping me out of my nostalgia. *"If Jack was here, he'd have you locked away, probably in a basement somewhere...or in a coffin. You've been taking the high road all your life. Don't you start going for the low-hanging fruit now."*

"Yeah, but where has the so-called high road gotten you?" That other side of me was surfacing again, the Devil's advocate known as Shady Chick. *"If it's the best route, then*

why are you sitting in the parking lot of a building you just got tossed out of wondering what to do with your life?"

It was time to get out of that parking lot. If I sat there and listened to these two warring thought patterns any longer, I'd be spiraling back into regret over the last ten years of my life and headed for a stay in a psych ward.

I started up my car and quickly wiped a rogue tear from my cheek. As I was about to back up, there was a knock on my driver side window.

"What the hell are you doing in there?"

It was Issa. I just sat with my hands on the steering wheel and looked at him. He stared back at me with one arm resting on my car's roof, his head cocked to one side, and his eyebrows raised in defiance. He didn't even really have to bend over much to see me, because he only stood about a foot taller than my compact Chevy.

I had been avoiding him for a few days, parking my car where he couldn't find me and pulling extra overnight hours at my old job at the museum.

"What are you doing?" he insisted.

"You said you didn't want a roommate." I said as if he could hear me clearly from my rolled up window."

"I cannot hear a word you are sayin'. What the hell are you doing?" He shook his head in frustration and lowered his voice.

He knew raising his voice always annoyed me. It was okay when it was low, with just enough depth to let me know that he was male, but when he raised it he sounded like a squawking goose.

"Roll your window down... roll the damn window DOWN!"

I placed my hand on the window crank and slowly rolled down the window while staring at the brick wall directly in front of my old parking space.

"Decrease!" he yelled

"You said you didn't want a roommate." I responded.

"DECREASE!"

"Why don't you decrease your volume? And you can't double park behind me in this lot! You're not a tenant here."

"Neither are you!"

"These people don't know my business. You tryna make it known to every damn body!"

"I will NOT hold your foot!" He shook his finger at me to emphasize how serious he was in uttering this Liberian expression, one which was supposed to assure me that he had no intention of begging me. He was already begging.

"Your pride," he sucked his teeth and continued, "… your pride is too much!" he yelled.

"You said you didn't want a roommate." I repeated calmly.

"I told you that stuff about roommates a long time ago, before this! TURN ON THIS CAR AND DRIVE TO MY PLACE!"

He was right. I could feel the ache of pride all over my body as if six dogs were latched onto my limbs. And I was feeling all kinds of upset over needing his help. The last time I needed a man's help like this, it ended in disaster. But I could improve my situation a lot quicker if I accepted his assistance. It would help him, too.

I slid my hand down to my keys and slowly turned the ignition, completely dropping my chin into my chest in defeat. After that, I took a deep breath and lifted my head again to face him.

"You are insane." he said pointing his own ignition key directly at me before getting into his car and heading back to his place.

3

The first statement posed to me during the deposition the next day was, "Please explain this… recent eviction."

"Well," I said, "I hired an attorney as part of my bankruptcy filing, to help me negotiate more reasonable terms on my student loans, because $1200 per month is just impossible. It seemed like the only choice I had after exhausting all other means of adjusting the monthly payments and getting nowhere after asking you guys for reductions. I figured at least you would know that I was making an effort to find a viable solution. I didn't wanna just say 'forget about it'. But, of course, an attorney has to be paid, too. His retainer set me back two months rent. I thought I'd be able to catch up, but it didn't work out that way."

"And you thought suing the government would look like a good faith effort to repay your debt?" the attorney for the private student loan titan, Ellie May, asked.

Suing the government? That wasn't what I was doing. I was baffled and rendered speechless by her question, but I figured she might know more about these things than I did.

I leaned in to my attorney, Mike, and asked, "What the heck is she talking about?"

"What do you think is implied by the term *Adversary Proceeding?*" he whispered quickly, then turned back toward the other side.

"You never told me this was a *law suit.*"

"It is...don't dwell on the terminology. They're just trying to intimidate you."

"That's really gonna bite me in the ass." I mumbled to myself. "They've been pretty adversarial towards me. I'm just trying to get out from under their feet! *I'm suing the United States government?*"

He covered his mouth and whispered yelled, "Look alive!"

Never in a million years had I thought of it that way. Somehow, my research and desperate, scatter-brained thinking on the problem had left me with the impression that an Adversary Proceeding was a simple legal tool. I thought it was a last resort for getting favorable results where bankruptcy alone would have no impact on my student debt. I thought it was some sort of addendum in my bankruptcy case— not an actual law suit. Legalese was so often counterintuitive. I didn't realize it meant "legal combat".

Mike folded his arms and rubbed his beard calmly while looking ahead as the other side continued abruptly.

"Ms. Luck, your take home pay with the bank is $30,000 a year?" The attorney for Atlantic Tuition Services asked.

"Yes." I said

"You're bringing home about $2500 per month, correct?"

"I am now. I just started the job a couple of weeks ago. Before that, my internship only paid about nineteen 'k'." I responded.

The attorney for Atlantic Tuition Services stuck his chin out and squinted his eyes at me.

"Nineteen 'k'... nineteen thousand? That's—"

"Ten dollars an hour. Around sixteen hundred a month. I worked there for 2 years."

Though my answer seemed unbelievable to him, they had all my financial records in front of them to prove it. And I assumed these were the kinds of people who should know full well just how crappy internship pay could be. I was sure many of their friends and colleagues had benefited greatly from unpaid internships, the types of golden opportunities that kids like me couldn't afford.

He went on, "My understanding is that the possible salary range for someone with your credentials is between $40,000 and $50,000."

I nearly choked on the water I was sipping and quickly apologized for spewing on the secretary across from me.

"I think you have the figures for someone who is already a *licensed* architect. I was an intern before the layoffs. And if there were any architectural intern jobs to be found now, they would pay something closer to what I'm making at the bank. That's how much they'd pay me, anyway. But, as you should know, those jobs are pretty much gone now."

Another attorney, the one representing Ellie May piped up, "Well with what you're making now, it seems that you could definitely cover your monthly expenses with Ellie May.

"Right," I said, "but those are not the only loans that I have. The reason the Atlantic Tuition Services attorney is also here is because I have a monthly obligation to them as well. And you *all* have been threatening me regarding immediate payment, so..."

I stopped and took a deep breath, wondering when my attorney would stop trying to look tough and provide some input. He shuffled through his papers, seemingly still trying to figure out his plan of attack. The dangly curls at the sides of his head shook as he moved around, eyeballing different pages.

"In total, my monthly student loan obligation is nearly half my monthly income." I went on. "With my recent eviction, I'm having a harder time finding a place. I'll stand a better chance of getting into a place that is at least safe if I can offer around six months' rent up front, because, obviously, money talks."

"But haven't you already secured a new living arrangement?" the secretary from Ellie May interrupted.

Mike finally responded. "That is not an ideal living situation, just a temporary one. She was just living out of her car a little while ago. A-and it's beside the point. It is unreasonable for you to expect anyone in her shoes, e-especially a recent graduate, to cough up $1200 a month in student loan repayments."

One attorney sat back in his seat with a sigh while another one folded his arms.

Mike continued, "Eh, this whole thing of saddling 18-year-olds with ridiculous amounts of debt that can never be forgiven is downright suicidal for the society. You know it is. Nobody expected *your* generation to take out a mortgage on their lives for an education. It's ridiculous. If she had racked up this same $100,000 in credit card debt on shopping sprees, fancy living, or some defunct business, bankruptcy would have given her a clean slate by now."

As the attorneys and their assistants became visibly annoyed, Mike just kept going, waving his hands, looking down at his papers, then jerking his head back up to glance quickly at them.

"What you all are dishing out is punishment for doing exactly what she was supposed to do. This recession— which I'm sure is only the beginning of a huge mess— is due in large part to this very behavior by you banks. We all know the condition of the current economy. Surely something reasonable can be granted here."

I think he was starting to lose it. I could tell that he was an emotional guy from our first meeting, but I had thought that passion would help drive us toward the resolution that I wanted. Plus a win could be a boost for his career, since it would set a bit of a precedent. Adversary Proceedings were rare and nearly impossible to win. He had never had a case like this.

In the beginning, he seemed genuinely angered by my situation and wanted to help. In our first consultation, he kept using words like "extortion" and "usurious" to describe this Fourth Circle of financial hell that I'd gotten myself into. He even referred to Ellie May as the "Student Debt Mafia".

"Oh this is just an utterly usurious repayment plan," he would say. *"This type of debt slavery is just another way to lock Americans out of the very opportunities that college is supposed to afford. Why weren't there any student advisors with some financial know-how who could explain what all this would mean before you did it?"*

I doubted that even the best financial advisors would have been able to get into my thick head back then and talk me out of my pipe dream.

Mike was close to my age and a bit of a spiritual seeker in his spare time. Although he was Black, he had developed a deep interest in Orthodox Judaism by way of an Old Testament obsession. I figured that must have been why he was so fixated on the word "usury". The Bible was the only place I'd ever seen it.

I could only imagine what those people on the other side of the table were thinking while this wannabe Hasidic Black man in a yarmulke with little curled plaits in front of his ears lectured them about corporate greed.

I started to realize he had no idea how to pull off a win. The longer we worked together, the more I saw that he was just a little too much like me— young, still finding his way, and way too hopeful.

He started his argument strong enough but quickly devolved into looking down, gesticulating with his hands, and punctuating his words with "ums", "ers", and "ehs". I tried to remain calm and pick up where his poker face fell off. I looked straight ahead with my hands folded, and eyeballed the other side in order to keep us from looking like a total mess.

For the most part, the others kept their game faces on. They would all behave as if they knew nothing of the current economy or of the inherent ridiculousness of this entire situation. I was getting my first real adult lesson in the law— that it sometimes has very little to do with morality or common sense. I figured I'd have to wait it out while they all played their legal game, and then I'd spend the rest of my life as an indentured servant to them.

In that moment one thing became clearer to me than it had ever been. Getting that degree was the single worst decision I had ever made. Even though I had never rebelled against my parents, eloped, taken drugs, or done anything else that would have given me the label of "young and dumb", I had still managed to destroy my life right out of the gate. This was my brand of stupid.

My mother had been right. I should have quit long before now.

As they wrapped up their arguments for the day and I regretted not following a fleeting thought to just go to beauty school a long time ago, a reminder on my phone sounded off. It was time to take the test.

As everyone rose to leave the deposition I unconsciously lapsed into nice old Southern Jane, and I couldn't quite figure out why. I guess it was enough to feed my need to feel like these were humans I'd just interacted with.

One of them asked what was good for lunch nearby, and I mentioned some Chinese place up the street. I was looking them in the eye as they packed up and we brushed by one another. I sort of smiled at one or two of them, and even instinctively shook the hand of the attorney's assistant who sat next to me. The rest glanced at me blankly before saying, "Good afternoon", nodding dryly, or signaling goodbye with one of those half-hearted salutes.

"Why are you doing that?" Shady Chick blurted out within me.

Being polite and respectful, even in the face of disdain, was a bad habit that I had still not quite shaken. And, of course, part of me thought that not acting like a jerk here might help.

"You're making an ass of yourself." Shady Chick continued. *"You're already screwed. Kissing up WON'T help!"*

"Let this be a lesson to you," Mike said once they were all gone and my self-pummeling was in full effect. "Debt is bad. I know it's the way this country is run, but for someone like you, it's just another trap. Why in *hell* did your parents let you do this?"

"Wasn't their decision to make." I said.

By now he seemed annoyed and a little angry. So was I. I just glanced at him with barely an expression then kept packing up.

"I had a look at that lease you signed," he said. "Do not *ever* sign anything like that again. You waived your right to a jury trial."

"Right," I said, "because more court proceedings is exactly what I need right now."

"You gotta learn how to stand up for yourself *before* the you-know-what hits the fan. Save you a lot of trouble...You might have at least gotten some sympathy."

"And another bill from you? I doubt it." I said.

"I'll email you the next steps." he said.

We parted ways and I made a b-line for the ladies bathroom just down the hall.

I stepped into the black and brown marble-laden bathroom stall. Even the dividers were marble— no standard builder issue metal stalls here. But I wasn't nearly as impressed by this mini interior design wonder as I may have been some other time. I opened the pregnancy test and squatted over the toilet, coated the reader per the instructions and waited.

"Oh, come on!" I yelled impatiently.

I waited again, as if my demanding half-squat stance should be more than enough to get me a clear answer. The reader showed a faulty image of half a plus sign with the top and left portions completely missing. Then it just faded to white.

"Was that a yes?! Is this thing broken?!"

I had heard a couple of other women moving around in the bathroom. One was finishing up at the sink while the other sat in the stall next to me. They both fell quiet.

"Come ON!" I yelled, kicking the divider. "MOTHER FUCK! You STUPID piece of SHIT!"

"Miss, can I get someone to help you?"

It sounded like that idiot brunette who was taking notes for Atlantic Tuition Services during the deposition. She was the one who snickered when I itemized my monthly expenses and chose $0-$20 as the range for the amount of money that I typically spent on clothes.

"Girl, you know there's only one way you can help me." I said with a sigh. As she closed the bathroom door behind her I added, "but it wouldn't hurt if you KISS MY ASS!"

I didn't care anymore about appearances. I wanted to scream at the top of my lungs, throw up my hands like a superhero, bust right through that antique copper tray ceiling, and fly out of there. But it was clear that I had no superpowers.

I was totally enthralled in smashing the pregnancy test with my right heel when my phone rang. I kept smashing while I looked to see who was calling. It was my old friend Celine.

"Yes?" I answered.

"Wow. Some greeting. You sound like you're in the middle of somethin'," she said. She had no idea what I had been through that morning. She didn't know much of anything that was going on with me.

"Not really," I said with no desire to share or extend this conversation beyond a couple of painfully cordial minutes. Celine hesitated. I assumed that she could sense that my busyness wasn't the reason for my coldness.

"I just called to see what's up with you. Hadn't heard from you in a while."

A "while" was something like a year.

"I tried callin' a couple of nights, but you didn't answer. So I figured I'd try during the day even though you might be at work... how are things going with interning?"

"The bottom fell out." I said. "I'm sure you already know."

"Yeah, I'm sorry. I've talked to a couple of other people from school who are in design and construction and stuff like that. They say the banking thing is causin' problems for them too."

By now I was leaning against one of the marble dividers with my arms folded, feeling mixed emotions brewing. I wanted to end the charade right then, but I kept holding back, because Celine had seemed like such a good friend once. I didn't want to end it on a sour note.

A couple of years back, after I returned from Bermuda, she stayed at my place for the summer and then spent her senior year in a nice apartment on Wissahickon Avenue with her good friend Leslie, ten minutes down the street from me. She never once invited me over.

We only saw each other occasionally when she and Leslie caught a ride with me and my coworker, Emily, to our favorite church. One Sunday, as she and Leslie hopped into the back seat, they wrapped up a lively conversation about a movie they'd seen the night before. I hadn't planned to butt into the chat, but Celine apparently felt the need to include me in the recap.

"Oh, Jane, we went to see War of the Worlds last night. I thought about inviting you, but I figured you were prob'ly too broke or too busy to go."

Visibly appalled by Celine's rudeness, Emily mumbled, "What the — " just loud enough for everyone to hear.

I was, unfortunately, too exhausted from school and working two jobs and one hustle to dredge up an outburst that would do the situation justice. This was one of those times when I wished I had a temper that could take me from zero to psycho in a matter of seconds. At least it would have made me feel better.

Instead, I stepped out of my car, adjusted my seat forward, and calmly gestured for Celine to get out. She had no idea what I was doing, so I leaned in.

"I can help you out, or you can simply get the hell out of my car."

I stood back up, folded my hands in front of me, and waited. I didn't know if the look of shock on her face was due to the fact I was kicking her out of my car, that she'd heard me cuss, that she'd be missing church that day, or all three.

Emily turned around again and warned Celine and Leslie, "I don't think you want her to help you out."

"Jane!" Celine yelled while grabbing her purse. "WHAT IS GOING ON?! I didn't mean to offend you. It was just a joke!"

I nodded, got back into the car and drove off.

That had been our last in-person encounter about two years ago. I thought about calling her at some point to apologize and to explain what was going on with me during that time. But every time I thought about that, I remembered that she *knew* what was going on with me. I hated my internship, I missed Ali, I was floundering through my senior year knowing that my career was going south before it even had a chance to begin, and yes, I was broke. And then there was Jack. I was sitting at the top of a spiral slide and she knew it, but she didn't seem to care.

I resisted the urge to ask her how life in California was going for her and Leslie, but she volunteered to tell me anyway.

"Yeah, I still haven't landed my ideal job out here yet, but I've been doing some temporary styling jobs. I could care less about working with celebrities or TV shows, not that I've met any celebrities—I'm not looking to. I would prefer to design for a department store."

She had moved to California with the single intention of landing a job in the corporate office of a large clothing retailer. With her focus and determination, I knew she'd eventually do it.

"That's good," I said half meaning it and half rushing the conversation to an end. "Look, I gotta go. Still *busy*, you know how that is."

"Okay." She said. I could tell she was a little deflated.

"Alright," I said, "Well I hope all goes well with—"

"Have you talked to Jessica at all?"

"You mean has Jessica talked to *me*?"

"...It wasn't just you, Jane. When she got engaged, she cut everybody off."

"It wasn't because she got engaged." I said. "It was because she was getting ready to go to medical school and she thought she needed a new set of wealthier, more refined friends. She's a friggin' snob. Wouldn't even speak when she saw me on campus."

"Jane! I don't think it was that at all, and what's up with the language? She was just probably goin' through a lot of stuff." Celine said.

"Look," I assured Celine, "One of the last times I talked to her she was telling me about some classmate of hers who lived in one of those new river condos in Manayunk. She was talkin' about how the girl invited her over and greeted her at the door with a glass of wine. *'I need to find me some more friends like that!'* That's what Jessica *said*."

"Jane, I know you had a hard time after Jack died," Celine said, pissing me off by mentioning it. "It didn't help that things ended so abruptly between all of us. But things change, and I figured you'd be okay since Jack was crazy anyway and you had such a great life ahead of you! You just seemed stronger than all of this. I never wanted you to be as mad at me as you were at Jessica. It's not fun being on your bad side."

"Yeah, one less person giving you free stuff. Hey, *I* didn't put you on the bad side. You mosied on over there of your own accord."

"Well," Celine said with a sigh, "I hope things will be okay for you with the job and all. I think we all have a sort of tough road ahead."

"Tough ain't nothing new." I said.

"I guess I'll talk to you sometime." Celine concluded.

I ended with "Alright."

4

I was on autopilot again, massaging Issa's achy, flat feet without even a second thought as to why. He would ask me, so I would do it. He would come home after his 9-5 at the bank and evening hours in his cousin's restaurant and whine pitifully about his feet. Then for about ten minutes most nights before bed, I offered a massage.

Admittedly, I took some pride in giving a good massage. A friend or two had always complimented me on my ability to "tune in" to their pain and help alleviate it. It was my thing. The expression of tenderness was also a nice reprieve from our otherwise dull relationship.

I finished up, and before sliding under the covers I asked, "Why do I keep finding my little monkey shoved under this bed".

He glanced in my direction with the most disinterested of expressions then slid a shirt onto the ironing board.

"That thing gives me the creeps. I can't sleep wit' it staring back at me. Why don't you have a Teddy Bear or a Bunny or sometin', like a normal gal?"

"Mo-mo's not scary. He's a momento from my friends back home, an inside joke after we visited the zoo once and a gorilla kept staring at us and screaming whenever we tried to leave, like it didn't want us to go. It was kind of how we all felt when I moved away."

I poked out my bottom lip, danced the palm-sized plush toy with dangly legs in his face and said, "Please don't put me under the bed again. It's cold down there! Lemme keep you company!"

"You are hopelessly strange," Issa replied with a slight smile.

****

The next morning, we stepped into the cramped and grimey hallway just outside his apartment. The air coming in through an old, metal-paned stairway window was damp with morning moisture. It mingled with the decades-old carpet, resulting in a smell full of must, paint, and wet dog hair.

As I was beginning to succeed at ignoring the hall smell, an even more pungent scent came wafting out from under his neighbor's front door.

Issa turned to me with his index finger raised and in a very serious and indignant tone said, "That guy *ne-vuh* stops smokin'."

He lifted both his hands in a *"Who knows"* gesture.

"And I nevuh see him come out of there. I been living here for almost three years, and I only saw his face once.

Somebody told me he sells that stuffs, but I don't know how when he's smoking it all up."

"Stuff." I said.

He looked at me and waited to find out what I was talking about.

"You should say 'stuff', Issa. No 's' on the end."

"Okay." He turned his lip up at me then straightened his back and shoulders and grudgingly repeated, "Stuff."

"You get that language thing in check and they won't be able to touch you."

I could tell by the smirk on his face that he appreciated my advice. I tried not to impose it often, but sometimes he needed the reminder. His Liberian accent caused him to relax his enunciation of the ends of words, and there were times when he confused his plurals, saying things like *"we should cook some corns with the chicken"*.

"Is your boss still giving you funny looks whenever you speak up in a meeting?" I asked.

"No, not lately," he said.

I gave him a quick look over, knowing that there wasn't much more coaching that he'd ever need from me. His pinstripe shirt was crisp, his dark blue slacks were pressed and creased, and the Brodie oxfords that he'd cleaned and set out the night before were very sharp.

"The bank is only a pit stop for me," I said, "but it's definitely where you belong."

He apparently didn't want to belabor the point, but I knew my advice to look his boss and co-workers directly in the eyes was working. Issa would be a great financial advisor, he just needed to act like it.

He was still wagging his finger toward his neighbor's door when I asked, "Was that his place where it sounded like a brawl was going on last weekend?"

"No, that was the other one, down there." He pointed into the darkness which was the other end of the hallway and shook his head. Then in that exasperated tone normally used by much older people when they're complaining about rowdy, ne'er-do-well young folk he said, "I don't know these people."

We made our way from the second level to the ground floor and burst into the sun-drenched morning as if escaping a collapsing train concourse. We casually waved goodbye to each other and got into our cars to head for work.

As I started up my scarred but faithful car, I remembered that I still had some unfinished business to attend to. There was a Rite Aid not too far from us down the street.

"You might as well get that over with." the Receptionist said.

I stopped at the drug store and picked up two pregnancy tests, choosing two different brands for added quality control. I also stepped out on faith and grabbed my newly filled prescription for birth control from the pharmacy. If God saw fit to let me out of this jam, I wasn't going to pile one mistake which I was bound of make again (having sex with Issa) on top of sheer stupidity (not using solid protection).

I didn't have far to drive down the street to my alma mater in East Falls. Thankfully, I didn't run into anyone on the way to the bathroom in the fashion design program's main building. I wanted no repeat of that scene just after the deposition.

The results on both readers were negative, and that gave me an extra emotional boost. Maybe I could even get another by nailing this meeting I was headed to.

It was with Melinda Tyson, a professor whom Celine had formally introduced me to, but who I had also chatted with at a couple of events for Fulbright scholars. She was the only tenured black professor in the Fashion Design program. She also had extensive experience and connections across the spectrum of design professions.

The last time we bumped into each other she offered to tell me about some firms in the city that might be hiring interns. If I could get back on board with an architectural firm, I could break through the "secretary ceiling", do some real design work, and begin accumulating credits toward licensure.

I was happy that Professor Tyson had not just given me the contact names immediately. It gave me the impression that she wanted to sit down with me, get an understanding of my goals, and help me construct a plan for getting back into the field. A new potential mentor had finally taken an interest in me, and I desperately needed her insight.

When I got to her office I immediately grabbed my portfolio and put it on her desk so that she could give me feedback. She walked through the door and sat down without saying a word. She had a broad, toothy smile which accented her flawless mocha skin, but she was the kind of person who didn't smile often and whose grin (more like a grimace) garnered more suspicion than comfort. She flashed it briefly then said,

"Good morning, Jane."

"Good morning! Thanks for meeting with me."

I didn't waste time on fillers like, *"how was your weekend?"*, or *"isn't it a gorgeous day?"* She was a serious, professional woman who didn't have time for that. So, I greeted her and let her speak. She thumbed through my portfolio for a few seconds then stopped to look at my resume.

"You know," she said, "economic crises like this one really do serve a purpose, especially in your profession."

"Oh," I responded with genuine curiosity, "what would that be?"

"They help to eliminate the weak along with unworthy competition."

Ouch! I certainly didn't want to be considered one of the weak or unworthy.

"But that's not who you are, right?" For the last time during that meeting she let that smile slip through. "You've got what it takes— smarts, discipline, follow-through."

"Absolutely!"

If she could see those qualities in me, they must not have faded completely.

While still looking down she casually asked, "Do you have a church home, Jane?"

"Yes, I go to Zion Temple."

She slowly nodded in recognition of the name of the prominent megachurch then said, "My church has a smaller congregation, and I think you might really enjoy the Pastor's teaching. There's a growing young adult program. Would you want to check it out this Sunday?"

I thought it was a little odd that she was leading the conversation with a discussion about church, but I was willing to try something new. The pastor at Zion was recycling the same old shallow, pew-jumping, emotion-baiting sermons, and I was looking for more substantial teaching. I was more far gone that I'd ever been spiritually, and I needed more than feel-good messages.

"Sure. I'd like that." I said.

"Great!" She gathered my portfolio and papers and handed them back to me. "I'll pull together the information for my contacts. After church, I can give them to you. You can call them to set up some informational interviews to learn more about their work."

"Okay." I said. This wasn't exactly the meeting I had expected, but I thought a chance to interact in a non-professional environment could help us to get to know one another. I accepted her terms with a handshake and a closing "thank you".

I was sure to set up my first informational interview immediately. The next week, we met again in her office.

***

"So how did your interview with Mt Airy Design Associates go?" This time Professor Tyson seemed a lot more personable. She met me during her lunch break and ate a turkey sandwich while serving up a generous portion of smiles.

"It was great! I had a chance to meet their other interns. Each one of them gave me a short chat about the projects they're currently working on. The Principal, Dennis, gave me a thorough walkthrough and showed me the drawings and models for some of their best Center City work. They're working with B.I.M., Building Information Management software. We didn't have that at my last firm, so it would be great to learn it. My old boss used this really antiquated software called MicroSpot MacDraft— he didn't even use CAD. And MADA's office is gorgeous, by the way!"

"I know, isn't it? They're starting to do more historic preservation work in the neighborhood, too. I know you've lived there so you'll appreciate that." She said.

"Two of their interns will be moving on to other cities soon, so I'll be keeping in touch for openings."

"Good. Do you have one scheduled for Highpoint?" She asked.

"Yes, for next Wednesday."

"So what did you think of church Sunday?"

"I enjoyed it. Everybody was really friendly. The spoken word thing was similar to something that's done on youth night at Zion."

"The young adult program does things like that once a month, but it's more geared toward people in your age group, you know. It's not teaching for high-schoolers and college students. It's really aimed at addressing the issues young adults face. Sometimes there are performances, and sometimes they do their own thing in the sanctuary. The program was nice, but you really didn't get a chance to see how things are on a typical teaching Sunday. You up for another visit this weekend?"

"Uh, sure. I wouldn't mind that."

Actually, I thought she seemed unusually persistent with the church thing. When she talked about it she scrunched her brow in a serious expression and spoke more quickly, like she was trying to shove in as much endorsement of her church as possible before it became too obvious. I knew that game, because I had played it myself for quite some time. It's a stealth move to slip a shot of Jesus to somebody who you think needs a highly concentrated dose.

I had also caught a whiff of how desperate her church was to bring in a younger, more diverse crowd. Much of their intimate congregation had already begun to die off, and there was only a handful of bored-looking young adults to accompany me during my visit. Maybe as a college insider, Professor Tyson had been tapped as a resource for church recruitment.

I wondered what this had to do with our professional dealings. I didn't mind one more visit, but I, frankly, hadn't found her church much more appealing than mine. I tried to steer the conversation back to my primary concern.

"So did you have any feedback about my resume and portfolio? I emailed them to you in a pdf file, like you asked."

"I did look at them." She said. She wiped her mouth with a napkin then took another bite of her sandwich. "I figured we can really dig into that after you do your other interview. Then we can consolidate what you learn from your visits and tailor your presentation materials to that."

"Okay." I said feeling a little confused. I didn't want to ask for too much, but when she asked me to bring those materials to her office the first time and offered to provide me with some "career mentoring" I had expected her to engage in more conversation about my actual career.

She continued, "You know, Jane, I think that as you continue visiting my church, you'll really find a home there. Right now, we're planning a mission trip to East Africa, and we'd love to have some highly motivated young adults there to help spread the message of Christ to the communities."

"Interesting." I said that calmly, but I could feel my temperature rising. I had never been a fan of mission trips.

I was becoming even more disillusioned with the idea of them after Issa told me about the Catholics who preached to the children of his hometown back in Monrovia while demeaning their culture and refusing to properly pronounce their names. He had told me a thing or two about all the foreign aid they brought with them in the form of clothing and other odds and ends. That steady influx of free goods had put a many local business people out of work.

Professor Tyson reached into a drawer in her desk and pulled out a pamphlet.

"Here's the information for it. They're shooting for Christmas of this year."

I must have been getting more annoyed with her advances than I allowed myself to admit. Before I had a chance to completely filter my thoughts I blurted out,

"Will we be getting into a more profession-oriented discussion?"

"Oh," I thought immediately afterwards, *"that wasn't so bad. Not disrespectful at all."*

I continued, "I have a few questions about my cover letter, and I'd like to refresh my portfolio with a new theme."

Professor Tyson looked at me for a few seconds without moving. Then she put her drink down and said, "Of course." She wiped her hands with her napkin and pushed out her chair to stand.

"I have a meeting soon. Why don't you email me your availability for the week following your next informational interview, and we'll go over everything then."

She extended her hand for a shake and gave me that hard-assed facial expression, which seemed a bit contrived this time.

"Will do." I said. "Thanks for your time."

Somehow I knew that I wouldn't hear from her again. I would definitely keep my appointment for the informational interview with Highpoint, but I could just sense that she really wasn't interested in following up, wasn't really interested in me. I decided to drive down to Pelham road on the way home for a glance at "The Villa".

***

When I pulled up in front of the inspiring mini-mansion, the owner was running down the porch stairs with a hammer. He haphazardly tossed it on the ground and went to the side of the house where a hatchet was lying in the yard just outside the sunroom. It was unusual seeing him so amped up.

He grabbed the hatchet and bolted back into the house.

"What the heck is he doing?" I asked myself.

The dining room light was on and the curtains were wide open. I strained to look through the dining room into the part of the kitchen which was visible. Inside, the owner stood with the hatchet, poised to take a swing, but it looked like he was alone in there.

After a few seconds of what looked like contemplation, he started hacking away at the already worn original cabinetry.

"Poor thing." I said to myself. "Must be having a paranoid trip."

Then I noticed the 8 ½ x 11-inch piece of paper taped to the front door.

"Must've been taxes. They're kicking him out!" I said with a mixture of shock and curiosity.

As the hatchet freed one of the cabinet doors from its top hinge, it fell toward him. He punched it and stomped it furiously after it fell to the ground.

Before starting my car back up I muttered, "I feel ya, brother."

5

"Why do you need a mentor?"

"Architecture is the kind of career you have to be groomed for, Issa. Education isn't enough. It is essential to know someone who can help you understand and navigate the profession."

"But that lady's not an architect."

"No, but she's the closest thing I have to one right now. She's an experienced designer, she's worked with architects and other designers her entire career, and she has a lot of knowledge and connections. If I could have made a good impression with her, she might have forwarded me on to an architect she knows. You have no idea how hard it is to chase down an actual practicing architect and make them give a crap about some newbie."

"You want a teacher." Issa said, mocking me. "We spent nearly a decade in school being taught how to make a living, and you see where that got us."

"I can't teach myself what I don't know, Issa. Of course... maybe I'm just damaging my reputation by asking for help."

"Huh?" he asked.

"Maybe it's interpreted as a sign of weakness. She said something about that in our meeting. In this profession, needing help is kinda frowned upon. You certainly aren't supposed to admit it."

Issa froze and gave me a worried look. "She used that word?"

I bit my lip and stared at the wall in contemplation, feeling embarrassed and knowing that Issa could see it.

Maybe Professor Tyson was never interested in me because she didn't see any potential in me, none that was compatible with my goals. Maybe the fact that I needed so much guidance was yet another sign that I was way out of my league. Who else thought that? Clearly my parents thought that. Maybe my professors had thought it, too. Did Issa think that?

I wasn't ready to give in, to say it out loud,

"I'm not cut out for this."

There's more than one way to accomplish a goal, but I had tunnel vision. I was an expert in biting off more than I could chew. In that moment, I was still blind to the fact that I hadn't taken a balanced approach to achieving my dreams. I was too much of a zealot, had too much passion and not enough common sense.

I was like Icarus. I didn't know how to play the vast and safe middle ground between stratosphere and sea, but instead, insisted on flying straight through the clouds and had my flimsy wings melted clean off.

For a long time, I thought lust was the sin of which I was most guilty. Now it seemed that it was hubris at work— that dreaded pride. And falling flat on my ass was the punishment. Who in the world was I to assume that such a life, such an opportunity would be awarded to me? "Why do you need someone to validate your dream?" Issa insisted.

"I just need someone to help me salvage it, someone with heavy machinery. Besides, all the great architects had mentors."

"All the *famous* architects had mentors. And that's according to the tales they told you guys in school. You think every single person who's ever made a niche for themselves in that profession did it by way of the same exact model? You're not a privileged kid, Jane. You need a back door method. Plus mentors are human. Mentorship is about attraction, not just smarts or potential. Someone who likes you will take the time to mentor you. No attraction. No one cares."

"Who you tellin'? Wait, what do you mean, attraction?"

"A connection," he said while clamping down on a piece of half-stale ciabatta bread and yanking the excess from his mouth. "Ya know, they like you. You remind them of themselves or somethin'. Why does anyone like anyone? They have to want to be around you. Otherwise, what's in it for them?"

"Attraction? That's exactly what I was trying to avoid."

As I leaned against the wall and slipped into my memories, Issa quickly gathered his bread, cup of water, and his book in order to move into the living room and away from me.

"*Attraction* was how it started with Jack." I said quietly.

Issa flung his head back in frustration. "I don't wanna hear about Jack."

"I know. I'm not going to spiral, I'm just sayin'." I reassured him.

"I do not want to hear about Jack."

"I didn't talk about it for an entire year, Issa. This is my healing process."

"Heeealing proceeeeess." he mumbled to himself as he flopped onto the sofa and opened his book.

"What are you so irked about?" I asked. "You're not the one lyin' in a grave somewhere. You didn't end up sliding over a cliff and into a raging sea because of the woman you loved... or thought you loved... loved in your own sick twisted way... tried to kidnap. It really wasn't love at all, but maybe he thought it was."

I looked up and saw Issa repeatedly banging the book against his forehead with his eyes closed.

"Oh, stop it!" I yelled.

"Wasn't it self-defense?" he asked. "That man was deranged! You're talking about love? Some things need getting rid of."

"And why are you sitting around here eating bread and water? You can at least afford a meal. The fridge is nearly full. Make a sandwich!"

He calmly replied, "My stomach is not my boss." then kept chewing and reading.

I opened the fridge and opted for an apple before discovering a covered dish on the bottom shelf.

"Oh, what's this?" I asked.

The pot was a small cornucopia of West African delights: grilled fish with attieke, collards greens, akara, and a few slices of cornbread placed on top.

"Ooo, did you get this at your friend's party last night?" I asked.

"Yah." Issa said.

"Who made it?"

He kept reading as if he couldn't hear me. I was pretty sure I'd partake, but I still wanted to make sure the cook wasn't one of his associates whose home hygiene was questionable.

"Issa, who made it?"

"My cousin."

"Which one."

"...Fatou."

"Oh, okay." I said. "She seems cool."

I remembered meeting her at Issa's graduation. She was extremely quiet, and I got a sense that she didn't speak much because of a language barrier. I assumed it hadn't been long since she had immigrated from Liberia. She seemed nice enough.

"I'ma leave these greens alone, though. Ya'll cook the hell out of those things."

"That's how we do." he said in defense of his culture.

"That's how you boil the nutrients out?" I asked sarcastically.

"We don't want to feel like some kind of rabbits chewin' on raw, crunchy leaves." he said with a laugh. "That's some white man shit... Ay, make me a plate."

"Is that a request? The inflection doesn't indicate one."

He looked up from his book, flashed a smile and said, "Please."

I shoved the plate onto his lap while he clicked on the TV.

"Your mom raised a good woman." He said while cracking open his can of tea.

We had taken a trip to Woodland Avenue over the weekend and stopped in a couple of African stores that sold Nollywood movies. Due to the low budgets and limited acting and directing skills evident in some of them, I thought they were hilarious in a so-bad-they're-good kind of way. The messages usually held some substance, though, and they always sparked some interesting conversation between us.

This one, Miscarriage of love IV, was about a guy who was trying to juggle two different lives and apartments with two girlfriends who knew nothing about each other. At one point in the film, girlfriend one saw a scrunchie on his bedroom floor which she was pretty sure was not hers. She asked him about it and he made up some story about how she supposedly pulled it off and threw it at him after getting drunk at a party the night before. She fell for the tale and went to sleep peacefully just before he took a call from girlfriend two.

"How's your mom doin'?" Issa asked me.

"She's fine." I said.

"I still can't believe she married that criminal guy."

"Me either."

"When does he get out of prison?"

"A long time from now."

"You think she'll be safe?"

"Only time will tell... I certainly hope and pray so." I said.

"...Why do you women always stick with guys who are bad or who treat you bad?"

I was slightly surprised by his question, and equally irritated to hear it coming from a man who never displayed any particular interest in relationship cultivation.

"Why would a man continue to treat a woman badly?" I rebutted.

He kept quiet but raised an eyebrow and tilted his head slightly as if sincerely recognizing my point.

The fourth installment in the Miscarriage of Love series ended with a five-minute chase scene as girlfriend one brandished a machete and pursued the guy on foot through a village on the outskirts of the city they worked in— it felt like at least fifteen minutes. The credits rolled after she spent just as much time crying *"Why-oooooo?"* and rocking back and forth on a couch as a song from the movie's low budget soundtrack repeated, *"A Miscarriage of loooooove... A Miscarriage of looooooove."*

"If they play this song AT ALL in Miscarriage of Love V, like they did in I, II, III, and IV, I'm writing a strongly worded email to some Nollywood producers." I said. "There is no need to play a song every five minutes."

I rolled toward the right side of the bed and looked for Momo. Once again, he was not on my pillow where I'd left him.

"Did you shove him under this bed again?" I asked Issa.

I looked under the bed and sure enough, there was my little plush monkey, grinning sappily at me from the chilly, cheap, hard-as-a-rock carpet. As I bent forward, the cool air that hit the back of my thigh reminded me of how much I missed my old place.

In Issa's place, I wasn't free to walk around blissfully nude. I'm sure he wouldn't mind it, but I didn't want to give him anymore ideas than he already had. I'd have to settle for lounging in the tank tops and little cotton skirts that didn't make me feel like I had to cover up in my own residence, but they had to be tugged on every time I made a move.

When I sat back up on the bed and looked to my left toward Issa, he was sitting there staring at me with his penis peeking out of his boxers and casually draped across his thigh. He just sat there with one arm leaning across the top of the headboard and that same blasé look on his face as if to say, "This is it. You want it or not?" He never failed to use this very same signal each and every time he was interested in having sex. I'd just turn around, and boom—naked penis.

Sex with Issa wasn't anything to rave about, but all of this was still fairly new to me, and I held out hope that things would get better with practice. I decided to accept his offer, since I was ovulating and feeling a little more amorous than usual. My birth control was something I never missed a beat on when I had access to it, so I had already taken my dose for the day. And even though I knew sex with Issa would probably leave me as unsatisfied and frustrated as it always did, I figured it might at least propel me into a good wet dream. An orgasm in my sleep with a nice fantasy man would be better than nothing.

"Did you buy new condoms?" I asked.

"Yes I did." He nodded.

"What size?"

"The right size."

"Not Magnum, I hope! I'm not tryin' to be funny, but if one of those things slips off again, that's a wrap. It's a good thing that last one didn't get lost. That is not a problem I'm interested in having."

He just kept staring at me.

"Lemme see it", I demanded. I held out my hand as he grabbed one from his nightstand.

"… I guess that's alright." I said after stretching it over a few fingers in a cursory examination.

I relaxed my shoulders and softened my gaze before climbing onto his lap. I kissed his forehead as his fingers traced my sides. Just before approaching his lips, I stopped and looked into his eyes.

"Let's try something different." I said.

"What?" he asked, seeming only minimally curious.

"What we were about to try a few days ago but you reneged on."

"I have to go to work in the morning." he said, visibly annoyed.

"So do I!"

"Early."

"And? What?" I said as I scooted backward from his thighs to his lower legs.

"I have an important meetin—"

"Right." I said nonchalantly.

"…You are much better with your mouth than I am with mine." he said, complimenting my way of assisting with the condom.

"Yeah, I can tell by how much you hate kissing. Well, I'll let you off the hook for now but I don't forget."

Probably would just be another disappointment anyway. As we went through our usual song and dance— the culmination of which I could virtually set a timer to— I realized that I was not very sleepy, and that I would need more than the usual pillow fantasy to top me off and lull me to sleep.

In four-and-a-half minutes we would have transitioned through two positions and three speed adjustments. A properly fitting condom would eliminate the likelihood of interruption midway and provide for a smooth shift from missionary to reverse cowgirl for me. About two minutes after that I would be completely bored and unable to hide it, at which point he would initiate the switch back to missionary. Two and a half minutes later, he'd be stepping into the shower. He'd be fast asleep about twelve minutes after that...if my dreams didn't come true and this was like every other time.

I would have approximately twenty-one minutes to concentrate on programming my subconscious mind for an optimal dream and priming my muscles for optimal release.

"That's not enough time." I already knew it. *"You should have started this much earlier in the day."*

It was time to pull out the big guns, so I turned on my laptop at Issa's desk while he showered. If I stayed in bed while it booted up, he wouldn't notice that is was on and ask me why.

At first, I had only engaged this resource occasionally, early on when the shock of our boring sex-life was still fresh in my mind. Meeting people online had never been my thing. I had imagined that if I did, it would be through some nice, wholesome dating site like eHarmony, where I'd stumble upon a mild-mannered youth minister and meet up later at Starbucks for coffee and scones. Meetup.com wasn't even on my radar until I heard about it from a coworker, created an account in order to join some yoga groups and was promptly greeted in my inbox by a man calling himself Stephen.

Stephen claimed to be an attorney working for a Center City firm. I figured that was a persona and the kind of lying that must be typical in online connections. Whoever

Stephen was, though, his persona never failed to serve as a very good primer for my sexual appetite. We'd never met in person and never planned to meet. Though many of our conversations were of a sexual nature, many weren't, and the ones that hadn't been were just as interesting.

Issa got into bed and promptly fell asleep. Once he was in la la land, I figured no movement on my part could make him stir. So I got up and checked my inbox. In order to milk the experience for all it was worth and pick up in the exact state of mind that I'd left off with Stephen, I backed up a couple of messages and reread a conversation that we'd had after our first chat on the phone.

Jane:
I think
that sometimes,
face-to-face contact is a distraction.
An impediment to true intimacy.

We fail to hear because we're rushing to be heard, we talk over and interrupt each other.

We don't pause to fully contemplate what was just said.

We don't fully chew before swallowing—we just gulp the interactions down, so they are not as filling as they could be.

Touching, and preferences, and the senses all get in the way, sometimes.

That's why I enjoy writing messages, and often prefer it. You actually have to read all the way through what a person says. Maybe even do a little research to understand them better or to back up your rebuttal. *Then you have to write back in order to respond, crafting every word, touching every letter. The whole process forces us to be a lot more thoughtful, if we remember to be authentic and to extend the same respect and courtesies that we would in person.*

Stephen:
That is a very interesting take on modern communication. And I must admit, it's a bit moving. Most would say all the texting and email is impersonal... a watered down human interaction. That's the easy, popular explanation anyway. But the technology is only a tool and a reflection of who we are with or without it.

I can definitely also say that those times when I have met a lady friend in person, there was certainly much more chemistry in the introduction and in our interaction if our initial online "courting period" was longer.

What do you think would have happened if we had met in person first? I think things would have taken a totally different turn. We probably wouldn't even still be talking, because I probably would have come on too strong and you wouldn't have budged, and that would have been that. No chance for me to make up for it later. No explanation. No sending you a sexy pic to win you over...

Since the indicator showed that he was online, I sent him a message.

Jane: *Shouldn't you be preparing for a hearing or something?*

Stephen: *Stopped for a break... gotta play some time.*

Jane: *Oh, are your playmates keeping you entertained?*

Stephen: *A few of them are. Glad you could join the party. Where's Mr.?*

Jane: *Asleep.*

Stephen: *If you don't mind my asking, why aren't you more demanding of what you want sexually from your boyfriend? You clearly have the gumption.*

Jane: *No point. Rather not waste the time. He's not the trainable type… more like a human dildo… switching to phone…*

I got comfy under the blanket then resumed the conversation by texting after noticing that he had already sent me a picture.

Jane: *Hmmm, a little more cleavage in the rear shot this time. Nice! 5 days a week in the gym got you looking right.*

Stephen: *I have to work a little harder for mine, but you'll see when you earn your mid-thirties. From what I can see, all that you're showing off is still God-given at this point…though it is a wonderful gift.*

Jane: *You mean damn near forties? 38 isn't quite "mid" anymore, you know?*

After I sent that playful jab about his age, he sent another pic, a nude this time.

Stephen: *Since you're so at good remembering numbers, you got one for this? Guess…*

I burst into laughter and then noticed Issa turning slightly toward me.

"Oh, carry your behind back to sleep!" I whispered to him.

Jane: *I dunno... looks like nine, no, ten inches.*

Stephen: *Good eye!*

Jane: *I'm an aspiring architect. My brain has a built-in ruler.*

Stephen: *Soooo... Your turn.*

Jane: *Take whatever risks you want. No nudies from me, dude. Pics never die these days.*

Stephen: *Your face doesn't have to be in it.*

Jane: *Then how will you know it's me?*

Stephen: *I know what your hands look like. Use them.*

Issa rolled over for a second time, this time facing me, then he slowly leaned onto his elbow and rubbed his eyes.

"I gotta use the bathroom. What you still doin' up?"

"Sending a quick message to my attorney." I said. "He asked me for some info related to the bankruptcy resolution, and I just remembered that I have to send it to him before morning."

While Issa went to the bathroom, I decided to wrap up my conversation with Stephen. I did need to go to sleep soon, and I figured I had gathered all the inspiration I was going to get out of him without being lured into a porn shoot.

Jane: *Top off with one of your playmates. This is strictly sapiosexual.*

I was about to put my phone on the nightstand and lie down, but then, I caught a glimpse of myself in the mirror across the room. The large fan in the window above the couch was blowing my locs onto my right shoulder, and the hallway light made the skin on one side of my body glow just so. It was a striking contrast of gold-toned cinnamon and pitch darkness, and the hair thing made me look like I was in some amazing, earthy and edgy photo shoot. I couldn't resist.

"Aw, what the heck! That could be a really nice one." I said to myself before positioning my phone for a selfie and covering my face with a pillow. I sent it to Stephen.

Stephen: *Oh, playing fair, I see. The Mr. know you're lying there naked for me?*

Jane: *Don't flatter yourself. I always sleep nude.*

I heard the bathroom door open, tossed my phone onto the nightstand and settled under the sheets just in time for Issa to shuffle out in a sleepy haze. He glanced at me for a second then put his phone on his nightstand

"Phone call this late?" I asked. "Sounded like you were talking in there."

"Nah, just recitin' some new formulas." he said, scratching his head. "I musta left my phone in the bathroom earlier. It was on top of the toilet. Did you see it?"

"Ew! No. G'night."

"Night."

***

Adrift in a tranquil pocket of the Atlantic, we lay peacefully in each other's arms. I didn't know how we got there. I just knew that it was a miracle.

It had been nearly three years since I'd heard Ali's voice and now here we were together, unbothered on his uncle's old boat. Surrounded by sea, sky, and those towering limestone rocks which kept watch over us, we picked up right where we left off.

As he sat there with his arms around my waist and his chin on my shoulder, I could sense his feelings of happiness, of finally reclaiming something that was dearly missed. I felt the same, but I was also fighting back a strong sense of shame over what my life had become. Would I still be the woman that he held on such a high pedestal? Were the things that he admired about me— my mental focus and spiritual discipline— even true anymore?

I gave up fighting and rested in the peace of his presence. If he was there, it was because he chose to be, and that was enough.

I turned around to look into his eyes. Then, just beyond the boat a fuzzy image emerged. It bobbed slowly into my peripheral view and only faintly triggered my senses until it was too large to miss. By the time it was right next to the boat, we could both clearly see what it was. The sight of Jack's lifeless body floating by seemed to send a shock wave through me and Ali, jolting us out of our embrace and me out of the dream.

Suddenly, I was sitting cross-legged on Issa's floor, in the hallway where his desk sat. There was a man standing over me, not saying a word. I had never seen him before, and I could tell that he was concerned about something. He just stood there motionless, looking at me like he might have if I was some troubled guest on a daytime talk show and he was in the audience gawking and listening. That part of the dream ended almost as quickly as it started.

***

The next morning, Issa and I were awakened by the fresh aroma of blazing cannabis.

"Whoa!" I said. I sat up and turned my head several times in an effort to find an air pocket that wasn't tainted.

"He's been smokin' since last night. You didn't smell it?" Issa asked.

"A little, but it wasn't this strong."

"I could smell it well enough."

"Didn't keep you from sleeping well, though." I said. "A contact high must've been the explanation for your malaise last night."

He ignored me and went into the hallway, which was actually more like a small transition space between the main room and the bathroom. It had some built in shelves which also made it a closet. He reached for a shirt and started putting together an outfit.

"I had a weird dream last night about somebody in this apartment." I said.

"Somebody in the apartment? Like a break-in or something?"

"No, it was like… somebody who was supposed to be here… or like, somebody who wasn't hostile. It didn't feel like an intrusion."

"Well, what happened?"

"Nothing, really. He was standing right in front of the desk, and I was sitting on the floor just in front of him. He just stared at me for a few seconds and then the dream was over."

Issa paused for a moment then asked, "What did he look like?"

"He was kinda tall, medium brown skin, thick eyebrows. He had a haircut sort of like Steve Harvey. He looked very neat, but just a bit outdated. He was wearing this tan blazer with a burgundy plaid shirt and dark brownish tie underneath… and slacks… dark brown slacks."

Issa's bottom lip dropped a little, and he removed his toothbrush from his mouth.

"What did he say?" he asked through a slurry of spit and toothpaste.

"He didn't say anything."

After rinsing his mouth, Issa returned to the bedside and sat down. He laughed a little then shrugged his shoulders as if shaking off a deeper thought.

"That sounds like something my dad used to wear." He said.

"What? Really?"

"*How* tall was he?"

"Taller than me. Like around six feet, I guess. Slim but a little beefy in the chest. Oh, and he had this tiny, crescent-shaped scar above his upper lip. He didn't look like you. Well… maybe a little around the lips and cheekbones."

Issa looked back at me as if shocked.

"He was Nigerian." he said.

Issa looked me in the eye with an expression of mild disbelief, then turned away.

"The scar... that was my dad."

"He didn't look happy."

"Hmm... that's really strange... Why can't you ever dream about me winning a million dollars! It's always bad stuff or strange stuff."

"Can't be bad if it's a warning that saves our butts." I said.

He stood up and resumed his dressing routine in silence while I hoped for a quick and easy answer to this puzzle.

6

Once in the office, I settled at my desk with the same renewed sense of optimism that I drummed up every day in order to make my new legal secretary job tolerable. By eleven o'clock, though, I was miserable as usual, struggling to focus on editing whatever business loan document or commercial lease I had been assailed with. As usual, I was hoping neither of the attorneys I assisted would catch me nodding off during one of the many disinterested stupors that I had to fight off during the day.

I never meant to take cat naps at my desk. It always happened when I least expected it. I'd be typing or collating or checking messages while coaching myself along, reminding myself of the growth potential the job offered, encouraging myself with little affirmations:

"This is a new and unexpected opportunity, a gift..."

"I am capable of adapting and thriving..."

"My possibilities are endless..."

"I am honing invaluable corporate knowledge and ski—"

Crack! My hand would flop down onto my keyboard or my stapler would fall out of my hand and hit the ground, suddenly waking me up.

"This can't be fun for them either." I said to myself as I watched all four of the attorneys I worked for file out of their offices, one by one, and trot to the break room for their third pot of coffee. Every one of them would need at least three more additional cups to make it to five o'clock. I refused to taint my body with that much caffeine and sugar.

John Ashton was the first to swing by my desk after getting a hit of the mid-morning brew. His voice was still a little groggy. He was always the first to arrive in the morning and always seemed the most concerned, the most courteous, and the most tired. I wondered if there was a correlation.

"Hey, Jane. How are things coming with the leases for those two gelato shops?" He asked.

"They're finished." I said. "I was just printing them out for you now."

"Great! I'll have you send those out, and then I need you to check flights for that trip I'm taking to the conference next month."

I nodded as he gave my desk an affirmative tap. I was careful to hang on to every word, because he spoke so fast his words almost ran together, and he finished up the conversation while hustling back into his office.

"Ya did a great job on those leases last week. You're getting good at it. There's a lot of room to grow here, so you could carve out a real niche for yourself if that's what you're interested in."

The next one to pass my desk was Emmitt Naylor. I'd been assigned to him as well, but he rarely had any work for me to do. He preferred to keep his door closed for much of the day, edited his own documents, and sorted his own mail. The most I did for him was relay lots of phone messages, most of which he didn't seem to care about, since he took all his important calls on his direct line.

"Did Peter Riseman call about that stupid Polar Plunge again?" he said while eyeballing a sticky note that I handed him.

"Yep, this is his fifth call."

He sipped his coffee and shook his head.

"Tell him I'll get back to him."

"Why don't ya just tell him to buzz off, Pete?!" Lynette Silverstein was another assistant who's desk was right next to mine. She worked for different attorneys and our cubicles were separated by a five foot divider, but she would jump in and help me out whenever she thought she needed to. Peter turned to face her.

"The guy's such a pain in the ass, but he's gonna be at that conference next month, and we're gonna be discussing a deal."

At this point, Lynette was standing up on her tip toes with her chin resting on her forearms at the top of the divider. She just shook her head, gave Peter a dissatisfied look, then sat back down.

Gerald Ackerman slid by Peter with two cups of coffee and gave a quick "Hello" as they both returned to their offices. Gerald was usually coolheaded, rarely seemed bothered by anything, and though he often wore a pleasant smile, he was a bit obnoxious in general.

Once, he was talking to me about his daughter who was following in his footsteps and going to law school. Apparently, she and I were close in age— a detail in which I wasn't the least bit interested. He had stood next to my desk for nearly five entire minutes rattling on about a wedding that they had just attended with some family friends.

"Nearly six hundred guests! I don't even wanna think about paying for something like that. Good thing Marissa isn't thinking of settling down any time soon. We're really proud of her. She's going to Penn, our old alma mater. She's in her mid-twenties, like you. Well, actually, she's nothing like you."

Gerald was content to let his business loan documents pile up on any given day. He seemed to have a knack for prioritizing, getting the important work done and not sweating the small stuff. But he had an important document to finish before going on vacation. I was happy that he didn't stop to chat.

The last attorney to stop by my desk was Deana Bell.

"Thanks for the file sorting, Jane." She said.

"No problem." I said.

"You know, I'm only going to be here for another week." She continued while thumbing quickly through a pile of documents.

"Oh, no! I didn't know that."

"Yeah, I put in my notice about a month ago. I'm giving my official goodbye tomorrow. I wanted to tell you because I'm going to be moving to West Africa to work with the African Development Bank in Liberia. I'll be assisting with the recovery efforts."

"Whoa!" I sat back in my seat quickly and tried to figure out if I should be really happy and intrigued or extremely concerned. Liberia's second civil war had ended five years prior, and the country's condition was far from stable.

"Your boyfriend is from Liberia, right." She asked.

"Yeah…have you been there before?"

"No, this will be my first time, but I've been in contact with my network there and aware of the conditions for quite a while."

"How'd you become interested in working abroad?"

"I guess I got the bug, like you did after that trip to Tanzania. You know I did an internship in Senegal right after undergrad at Cheyney U. I stayed connected with my friends there. Then this opportunity came up. I'll give you my contact information before I leave."

"Oh yeah! I remember you telling me about that. I'll check with Issa too. I'm sure you could use some of his contacts. His dad was a banker. I look forward to hearing good things from you!"

I stood up and gave her a hug as a show of optimism. From what I could see, she was a level-headed professional, and I hoped she'd have the wherewithal to navigate the shaky politics and tough economic climate which would make her job difficult.

Everyone got back to work in their offices, and I had gathered enough energy from chatting to make it through the next forty-five minutes until lunch. I was too curious about Deana's news to get back to work right away, though. So, I clicked on the Google window that was always open for my random daydreaming spurts, and I did a little research on the African Development Bank's country strategy for Liberia.

The time flew by faster than it had all day, and it was soon time to meet Issa for lunch. I waited in the lobby as he made his way down from the 30th floor Wealth Management department. Then I told him about Deana's new job as we walked to Liberty Place.

While the cooks at Au Bon Pain prepared my black bean soup, Issa hovered at the bread counter for several minutes then finally decided on a multigrain baguette.

"Issa, I swear, I cannot believe you're gonna sit here and eat a loaf of bread."

"This is all I need." He said as he cavalierly sliced and buttered the baguette.

"One of my attorneys is moving to Liberia. She's going to work for the African Development Bank."

"Oh yeah?"

"Yep. She'll be living in Monrovia."

"Serving under Ellen Johnson-Sirleaf, our first female president. Those women have something in common. Madame Sirleaf was finance Minister before the war." He smirked and continued, "We need some ladies to clean up the mess that was made. I hope that doesn't sound offensive."

He was poking fun, but I knew Issa was the kind of guy who could at least give a serious professional woman the respect due her work.

"Maybe they'll do an even better job than those other guys." he concluded.

"I don't doubt that Deana will be a great asset in the redevelopment efforts," I said, "but private capital always seems to do a better job of redevelopment and empowerment on the ground level. I wonder if her skills will be best put to use with a government-affiliated institution."

"Time will tell." He said.

***

When I returned to work, I checked my voice messages immediately. The first two were from a man who chose not to leave a name but only a number. He requested a call back from Deana and said the exact same thing in both messages.

"Please do not hesitate to return my call, as the matter is urgent."

Whoever it was had a strong Liberian accent.

My phone rang again as I wrote down Deana's message.

"Thank you for calling Arc One Bank Legal Department. This is Jane. How can I help you?"

"Yes, I'd like to speak with Deana Bell."

It was the guy with the heavy accent again.

"She's already gone for the day. May I leave a message for her."

"I have been attempting to reach her quite consistently today. The matter is urgent, however, I cannot divulge."

"Is it regarding her upcoming assignment overseas?"

There was hesitation before he answered, "Yes. Is there another number where she may be reached immediately — a cell or home number?"

I had been told, in no uncertain terms, that Deana did not want her personal numbers given to anyone calling on the general line under any circumstances whatsoever. She only gave them to colleagues, clients, and those who had been properly vetted. If he couldn't leave a detailed message to warrant my overstepping her directives, he'd have to wait.

"Her office number is currently the best way to reach her, but I can assure you that she checks her messages from home frequently."

There was a long pause on the other end. Then the man asked, "What is your name again, madam?"

"My name is Jane."

"And you are her regular assistant?"

"Yes."

"I recall Deana mentioning that her assistant has relation to some Liberians in Philadelphia."

"Yes, my boyfriend is Liberian."

"What is his last name?"

"Obi."

"That is a quite prominent family. They've made a name for themselves, particularly in our industry."

"I understand."

"Well, I don't want to appear rude, but I cannot go into too much detail over things with which you may not be familiar."

"That's not a problem. I have your number from your previous messages, so I'll be sure Deana gets them ASAP."

"Thank you, and Jane?"

"Yes?"

"What is your last name?"

"Luck."

"Ms. Luck, you take care." He seemed hesitant as he went on. "Especially if you can foresee a future with your boyfriend... The Obi family has affiliations which can make adjusting to the family... difficult."

"Mmm... thank you for that advice."

"You are most welcome."

I hung up the phone with a bad taste in my mouth. That last bit of advice was unsettling, but I was more turned off by his presumption that I may be considering a "future" with Issa.

7

After work, I was eager to tell Issa about what the man said and to get more in depth information about his family, which he had never really told me much about.

He spent almost ten minutes speaking in hushed tones on the phone in the bathroom before coming out and looking at me as if he was startled.

"What the heck is your problem." I asked while I undressed for a shower.

"I was talking to one of my brothers. He was giving me some news about the business back home."

"Is everything okay? You look upset."

"It's okay... You hungry? I have something."

"You cooked?" I asked in shock. "You can do that?"

"It's cabbage stew. It has chicken in it."

He looked distraught as he went into the kitchen, opened the pot and let me taste the stew. I could tell that he had something heavy on his mind, but I knew better than to press. That would only make him quieter.

"Thanks." I said as he spooned some of the stew into a bowl for me.

"I'm gonna take a shower." He said.

"*I* was gonna take a shower first! Oh, whatever." If the man wanted to take a shower to ease his stress I wouldn't stand in his way. Maybe he'd tell me a little about whatever was bothering him afterwards.

"Thanks for the stew." I said.

I sat down on the bed with my food and grabbed the remote control. After turning on the TV, I immediately noticed that Momo was, once again, not on my pillow where I'd left him.

I reached under the bed for him but didn't feel anything. I sighed, placed my food on the nightstand and got down on all fours to look under the bed. Of course, there was Momo, staring up at the underside of the bed. There was a random bill next to him, which must have fallen on the floor by mistake. I picked it up and opened the nightstand drawer to put the bill in there.

When I opened the drawer, I saw one of those beautiful, handmade birthday cards addressed to Issa. This kind of crafty stuff was right down my alley, and I picked it up to admire it.

The message inside was written in Liberian Kreyol. His birthday was back in the spring, and I assumed he was keeping the card because it was given to him by some dear family member.

It seemed I was right, because under that card was another old birthday card, two Ramadan greeting cards, and four Thinking of You cards. The strange thing was that they were all from Fatou.

"Why would his cousin be giving him Thinking of You cards?" I thought.

I mean, a strong family bond was one thing, but this was borderline romantic. With the advice of Deana's suspicious caller still in the forefront of my mind, I continued to inspect the drawer. Beneath the first stack of cards and a few bills was another stack of cards. These included several birthday cards from previous years and Valentine's day cards which were still inside their torn envelopes. The postmarks showed that the ones in the second stack, which were older, had been sent by Fatou from Liberia.

One of the Valentine's day cards contained this simple message,

"I love you now and always, Issa." -Fatou

There was also a picture inside the card. In it, Issa and Fatou sat on the couch in front of the window with the large fan just behind them. I looked closely at the expressions on their faces and could immediately tell that the vibe between them was not familial. They sat closely with his arm over her shoulder and her head tilted slightly in his direction. The look in his eyes was airy, almost sparkly, and his demeanor seemed particularly gentle.

I couldn't see any of my belongings sitting on the table, so I wanted to assume the picture had been taken some time ago. Then I looked in the corner of the picture and noticed one of my indigo, microfiber throw pillows tucked under his arm.

I scrambled around the room trying to find any other evidence before Issa surfaced from the shower, as if the picture and the cards were not enough. Then I remembered the stew.

I turned on the kitchen light and took a second look at the pot. It was not mine. And it definitely wasn't his. It was that same blue speckled pot with the matching lid that he'd brought home from Fatou's place after his graduation. And that was the same pot that the food we had the weekend before was in, even though we had returned it Monday.

I laid all the cards on the bed along with the picture and waited for him to come out of the bathroom. He walked out.

"You got me laying up in here, eating the bitch's food, sleeping in the same bed she's sleeping in, next to the little shrine you been keeping with all of her cards!"

"What?!" he said.

"You know what I'm talking about, so don't try to play stupid."

He looked down at the cards then back up at me with a sigh.

I got up and went to grab my suitcases from the closet-hall.

"Sit *down*! Jane, what are you doing?"

"I'm either getting out of here, or I'm kicking your behind. Which do you prefer?"

"Stop acting crazy! I dunno what you think you saw, but that's not what you saw."

"Oh, really? Valentine's day cards from your so-called cousin? You have cards in there from the nineties. You didn't keep anybody else's cards, Issa. Just hers!"

"Sit down for a minute." He let a chuckle slip and tried his best to dismiss what I had just figured out.

He tried to snatch a pair of pants out of my hand as I threw them into my suitcase. My arm flew up into the air as I jerked the pants back, and then I hit him in the head.

"When was the last time she was here? I guess she didn't see my suitcases behind the curtain in here. How'd you explain the shampoo plus conditioner in the shower—pampering your bald head?!"

"Why don't you calm down!" he said. "You're not going anywhere at night."

"You don't need to worry about where I go!"

He grabbed me from behind in a tight hug and held my arms down at my sides.

"Let me go." I said in a lowered voice.

"Sit down."

"Let me go, Issa.

He looked around at me, still holding my arms.

"You think it's funny?" I said.

"It's not this serious, now will you sit down?"

I stared back at him and took a deep breath before he released his grip on my arms. As soon as he did, I head butted him in the nose.

"Ahhh! Dammit!"

"Keep your hands off me!" I said as I finished stuffing one of the suitcases. I had been living out of them for the past couple of weeks, so there wasn't much to pack.

"She's been coming over here all this time, even before I moved in, I bet. The bitch probably knew about me, too. She'd have to be stupid to see all this stuff in here and not notice!"

He took one hand off his nose to point at me. "Do not call her a bitch."

I turned to face him. "Oh, you don't want me to refer to your lil' ho as a bitch?"

"Do NOT call her names!"

"Shut up!" I yelled while hurling oranges at him from the kitchen as I gathered my cooking utensils.

With all the commotion between us I almost missed a faint knock on the door.

"Who the hell is that?" he said with disgust.

"I dunno." I said. "Not my place, not my problem."

As I packed my dishes I heard what sounded like Issa trying to shush someone at the door. I walked into the main room to see what was going on.

"We have got talk in person, already. What happened to your nose?" I heard her say. Her voice was soft but tinged with some alarm.

Issa, holding a bloody rag to his nose, looked at me then back at Fatou.

"Hello." I said matter-of-factly. I stood tall with my hands on my hips, relishing the fact that I was the tallest one in the room.

"Who is she?" Fatou asked him with a raised voice.

He glanced back and forth between us as if he couldn't find any words to explain. So I helped him.

"I'm the woman you met at his graduation last year, the one who's been living with him for the past two weeks and dating him off and on for the last two years. I've just discovered that you are indeed *not* his cousin."

"Cousin?!" She asked, baffled. "Are you kidding me? You have a live-in girlfriend and you told her I was your cousin?"

"Not any more though, I was just moving out." I turned to go back into the kitchen. By the sound of it, Fatou resumed his ass-kicking while I got the last of my dishes and slung them into a Hefty bag. At that point, I was pretty sure she was a solid chick who didn't know about what was going on between us until just then.

"Excuse me!" I said as I moved toward the door with my suitcases, heading for my car.

He stood in the way blocking both of us and said, "Stop it before you get too worked up! You'll hurt yourself."

"Oh, now you wanna worry about me?!" Fatou yelled. She tried kicking him every time he came near her. He'd back away. She'd brace herself by placing her hands on the door jambs, and when he moved toward her, she'd jump up and try to kick him. The sight was pretty comical, since she was only about five-foot four.

"I'm worried about the baby!" He blurted out.

That stopped me in my tracks momentarily.

I moved my largest suitcase into the hallway and looked back at him. I had no words, only disgust. It was a disgust that I had always felt to some degree with him, so none of this really came as a surprise.

The yelling and kicking continued as I made two trips to my car and back into the apartment for my last load of belongings. Before I finished packing my laptop, two cops came walking up the hallways stairs looking straight into Issa's place.

"Who called the cops?" Issa asked. "This place is a marijuana plantation, but a working man gets into a quarrel and it's time to call the squad!" He shook his head in frustration.

I tried sliding by everyone and going downstairs to my car.

"I am not involved here." I said. "The dispute is between them."

"I'm sorry, miss," One of the officers said, "but until we know what happened, we need you to stay put."

The second officer was a tall, stocky man with medium brown skin. He smirked, huddled next to me and tried to lighten the mood.

"That guy's your boyfriend?" He asked me.

"Was."

"Were you here first?"

"Apparently not." I said.

He looked Issa's five-foot-six frame up and down as the other officer questioned him, then he turned back to me and said,

"He's a little guy... Good riddance."

The other officer motioned for Fatou and me to approach him and explained why they were called.

"One of the neighbors heard the fighting. He said there was a pregnant woman here and lots of screaming going on. He thought somebody might need some medical attention. Would that be you?" he asked looking directly at Issa. "It doesn't appear that either of the ladies are injured, but you're a bit bloody."

Just then, a door down the hall creaked open. A thin, young guy in baggy jeans and a dingy black ball cap walked down the hall and towards us. He stopped in front of the stocky officer and looked around him at us. I was pretty sure he was the one who was having the weed fest for the last few months.

"We must have been pretty loud if we could interrupt his high." I said.

"Um, I'm sorry man." He said to Issa with a worried look on his face. "It sounded like ya'll needed some help over there, and—"

"I don't need any help from you, man." Issa said, growing visibly angry.

"Yeah, but it sounded like you needed some help over there and I jus—"

"I don't need no help from you." Issa snapped.

The young man looked at us all, then just turned to go down the stairs.

"Sir, why don't you calm down and tell us what happened." The first cop said.

Issa told his side of the story. I sat on the couch and decided that when they made their way around to me, I'd keep my words to a minimum. I looked at Fatou who was looking steely with eyes blazing and arms folded.

The larger officer realized that, though Issa seemed to need it most, he was not interested in their help.

"I'm guessing you don't wanna file any charges or anything." he said.

Issa shook his head slowly. "No."

"Alright...well, you might wanna get that nose checked out. And how bout you two? You think ya'll can go your separate ways peacefully or do whatever you gotta do without anybody getting hurt any further?"

I held up my computer bag and said, "All I gotta do is walk out."

Fatou waved her hand in a dismissive gesture toward the officers then sat back in the chair with her arms folded again and her head turned.

"Well, I hope everything works out. You all take care."

They both turned to leave. I walked right behind them. As I turned a corner on the stairs, I looked up and saw Issa staring back at me. What for?

8

I sat in my car and waited for the cops to pull out behind me. I just needed to decompress for a minute. The cops began to drive off but pulled up slowly next to my driver's side and rolled down a window. The one who thought he had such a great sense of humor peered out from the passenger side and into my car.

"Might seem like a hassle now," he said, "but you'll save yourself a lot of trouble later."

After they drove off, I closed my eyes and took several deep breaths.

"This is what you should have done two weeks ago." I said to myself.

I turned the car on, adjusted my rear view mirror, and started looking forward to a night in a moderately nice hotel where I'd have a queen bed all to myself.

I couldn't help but ask myself that dreaded question that I had avoided month after month while I dated Issa:

Why? Why had I been so determined to keep trying with him? Or, rather, why was my resistance with him so low?

The only logical conclusion was that after falling for and losing Jack, then falling for and losing Ali, I had no idea just how vulnerable I was, how much my desperate desire for a companion was driving my actions. It didn't help that my friends in Philly had flaked out just when I needed them most and that my entire identity was crumbling.

As I turned my headlights on, out of nowhere two cars came screeching up next to me. Each one parked on a slant to block me in.

I looked around quickly and saw a man run up to my passenger side door. He tried to open it, but it was locked. By the time I looked back out the driver's side window there was a second man standing there with a handgun pointed straight at me.

I looked up at the face that was shrouded in darkness and saw his index finger placed over his lips. Both men were silent.

"Where are the cops! They were just here!" I thought.

I wanted to scream but I was too afraid to roll down my windows. If they just wanted to steal my car, they'd have no qualms about shooting me.

"But why would they want this raggedy car?" I asked myself. *"God PLEASE tell me that all they want is this car!"*

They were still not making a sound. The one to my left folded his arms and waved the gun in his direction in a summoning gesture. I looked ahead and tried to figure out what it would take to ram through the car in front of me. I could see another person still behind the wheel there.

Then I looked in my rearview mirror and saw that there was yet another person poised behind the wheel of the car behind me.

I gave in to the fact that a carjacking could be accomplished with a lot less people and no extra cars. They didn't want my car. I figured if they wanted me, they may be less inclined to shoot, at least right now.

So, I rolled my steering wheel furiously to the right and jammed the gas pedal down just as the guy to my right was pressing a center punch against my window. The glass broke with a quick pop as my wheels tumbled onto the sidewalk.

The relentless assailant punched through the shattered window and started climbing into my car as I tried to make it past the car in front of me, which had moved forward to keep me pinned in. I put the car in reverse to build up enough momentum to plow through it and ran right into the car behind me as it moved up. It was a pointless fight.

The assailant sat next to me with gun drawn, and reached across me to unlock my door. Then the man on my driver side, who had patiently waited out my failed escape attempt by standing in the street with his arms crossed, opened the door quietly and yanked me out. His Liberian accent was immediately recognizable when he calmly commanded the other man to,

"Park the car."

He led me to the entryway of Issa's apartment building as the remaining thugs casually parked all three cars. When they were done, I was led straight upstairs and back to Issa's front door.

"What do you want?" I asked them frantically. "You know Issa? I don't have anything to do with his family. I was just his girlfriend— actually we just broke up. I swear, I don't have any dealings with any of them... Did Issa put you up to this?!"

They all remained silent while the first one knocked on Issa's door. When Issa opened it, he looked at me and all four men as if he'd just seen the devil and tried to slam the door shut. The leader pushed against the door with the hand that was still clutching his gun and shoved his way in. Issa almost fell onto the floor as one of the henchmen pushed him into the apartment.

I sat back down on the couch where Fatou had sat before bolting into the bathroom. I could hear her sobbing.

Issa sat on the bed and stared at me with fire in his eyes.

"What did you do?" I growled at him.

"What did *I* do? Jane, this has nothing to do with your foolishness."

"*My* foolishness?"

"Now is not the time for you to use a bad situation to your advantage." Issa argued. "You're in cahoots with these guys over some stupid stuff I did? This is way over your head!"

"I have no idea who these goons are!" I insisted.

"I'm not the only liar here. You have some stories of your own."

"You know what, you one sorry nigga, Issa!"

"Did you just call me a nigga?" He stood up and tried to come toward me, but one of the thugs punched him in the stomach then pointed to the bathroom door.

"Go and shut her up." he said.

Three thugs stood watch while the main one sat down on the bed directly across from me. He tightened his grip on his gun when he saw me staring at it. Then he stood up when Issa got Fatou to open the bathroom door.

"Bring her in here." he said.

Issa and Fatou reluctantly came out and sat down on the couch next to me.

"Which one of you is pregnant?" the thug asked.

Fatou and I looked back and forth at the thug and each other. Did they want to harm the one who was pregnant, or the one who wasn't?

"Which one?" he insisted.

Fatou and I remained in shock, not knowing which answer would incur the worst consequence.

"Which one of you is carrying this dog's baby?!"

"Oh, that ain't me! That is not me." I said quickly.

However, I could see that Fatou had gotten her emotions under control long enough to lie and appear just as convincing as she feigned confusion and shook her head saying,

"No, no, no. I don't have belly."

Issa sat between us with pellets of sweat running down his face.

"One o' you bitches is lyin'." the lead thug said. "But we don't have a problem with killin' you both."

"Then why haven't you done it already?" I asked defiantly.

"What is wrong with you?" Issa cried to me.

I glared hatefully at him then looked back at the leader. I didn't want to prolong the inevitable, and speaking up to proclaim that I wasn't the pregnant one gave me just enough courage to say one more thing aimed at getting to the bottom of why we were in this predicament. I knew they wouldn't answer my question to our satisfaction or allow any of the power to be shifted to us, but I had to feel like I was doing something.

The lead thug simply opened the apartment door and motioned for the others to grab us all and escort us out. While we quietly descended the stairs, Issa pleaded with them to let me and Fatou go. "Do not hurt them." he said. "Do not hurt them, I beg. They are unrelated. What you want, they are unrelated. I beg." Never once did he ask them what any of this was about.

The leader oversaw the procession as we were escorted to the two cars that they had arrived in. Issa was led to the car that was parked in front of me, while Fatou and I were both led to the other. As Issa bent over to get into the backseat with the assailant's hand firmly planted on his head and a handgun nearly piercing the skin of his back, I could see that the expression on his face was one of guilt. "Sorry" was something I'd never heard him say, but I could see it in his eyes then.

I looked around at all the windows up and down King Street. Some were boarded up. Others were simply night blackened, and I hoped that behind one of them was at least one nosey neighbor, just one insomniac who might have peeked outside in a second of boredom and seen what was happening. I prayed that some plucky pair of college students would need to catch one of the late trains out of the Queen Lane Station and get suspicious upon spotting us. As I gave up waiting for the sound of sirens, I got into the car.

Then, seemingly out of nowhere, there were four gunshots. Fatou and I crouched onto the floor. I could feel the front end of the car lowering slightly as the two goons jumped out and looked around to see who had fired the shots.

"Somebody just shot out our tires." I whispered to Fatou. Tears began to flow from her eyes again, but she seemed afraid to make a sound.

All feel silent, and I knew now that it would only be a matter of seconds before someone dialed 911. But we'd still have to stay alive until rescued.

I raised my head to look outside and saw all four men hovering close to the two cars with guns drawn, still quiet as mice. While they waited I considered the likelihood that four seasoned thugs would carry out a coordinated kidnapping without extra weapons. I slowly leaned forward and lunged toward the first place where I thought another gun might be, then opened the glove box very carefully.

My hunch was right. I quickly took the gun out and gingerly closed the glove box. When I huddled back down on the floor with Fatou, she was holding back sobs with her hand over her mouth and shaking her head hysterically. Straining to see in the dark car, I pointed the gun upward and checked for a safety mechanism while praying that I wouldn't fumble and make matters worse.

As the standoff continued, I looked at the leader who was now just slightly bent over and slowly scanning his head back and forth to find the sniper. Then a lone figure emerged from behind Issa's building, standing straight up and facing us. As everyone focused their gaze on that figure, one of the thugs made a quick whistling noise to alert the leader that another silhouette had appeared about fifty feet away, near the intersection of King Street and Queen Lane.

There was no more time to waste if the assailants were going to pull off this kidnapping and avoid the cops. Two-by-two, they aimed their weapons at each figure. Just before they pulled their triggers both mysterious forms darted back out of sight— one behind Issa's building and the other behind the apartments fronting Queen Lane. When the thugs were good and shaken, more shots rang out from a completely different direction. This time the shots came from behind us. All four men ran and shot in that direction. Suddenly Issa jumped out of the first car, which immediately gave me the courage to do the same. I urged Fatou to exit the passenger side of the car, and I followed. All three of us huddled next to the car to avoid the barrage of gunfire. I could see that Issa and I had been thinking the same thing. He had retrieved a gun from the other car's glove box as well.

"Where are the cops?" I whispered.

"I have no idea." Issa said.

A look of disbelief came over his face as the shadow men reappeared and came running toward us all from each end of King Street. One of our assailants fell to the ground and began crawling, apparently shot in the leg. The other three thugs came back for us in an effort to salvage the mission. Before I could think, I was standing face to face with the leader of the thug pack. I raised the gun in a flash and shot him in the chest. He fell instantly.

It seemed I was sitting in the back of an SUV and speeding out of there with Issa and Fatou before I even had a chance to blink.

9

When I came to, I could see Issa leaning forward hugging a guy in the front passenger seat. The guy looked like Issa with the same radiant umber skin, and the same strong cheekbones and cupid's bow lips as the man who had visited me in my dream.

"Musa! You guys are lifesavers." Issa said. "What the hell is this? They are here already?"

Musa was Issa's oldest brother. I had never met either of Issa's brothers before.

I could faintly hear a gentle voice to my right which got louder as I realized the person was talking to me.

"Are you okay? ...Jane, how are you? Are you alright?"

Fatou's hand was on my shoulder. I looked down and realized that the gun that I'd shot the thug with was still in my hand.

"Give that to me." The man to my right said, softly. He held out his hand.

"Who are you?" I asked him.

"I'm Jelaney, Issa's cousin."

"Oh… I remember you. I remember, you were at Issa's graduation last year." I gave him the gun but pulled away suspiciously.

Jelaney was nice enough, but he had previously been introduced to me at the same time that Issa introduced Fatou to me as his cousin. I was pretty sure he knew that Issa was double dipping, and I didn't have much to say to him. I turned and looked at the driver, who gave Issa a quick dap then focused intently on the road.

"Who is that?" I asked.

Issa finally turned around and introduced the two men in front.

"These are my brothers, Baturu and Musa." Baturu waved from the driver's seat and Musa turned around with a 1000-watt smile.

"Are we going to the police?" I asked indignantly.

Though they all seemed protective, I couldn't help feeling like the odd woman out. They were all related, grew up together and spoke the same language. I was the crazy black American chick who was grossly out of the loop, had just broken up with one of them and then shot a guy. Whatever was happening, I didn't think they'd have any reason to be loyal to me for long.

Jelaney and Musa looked at Issa worried.

"Jane, we can't do that." Issa said.

"Why not? There is a dead guy lying in the road back there, and I killed him!"

"We don't know for sure that he's dead, and they're not going to go to the police. I'm almost certain they're here illegally. If we go to the cops now, they may detain everybody, and we need a head start on those goons."

"A head start? A head start to where?" I asked.

Issa placed his hand over his mouth and took a deep breath like he was trying to figure out the most delicate way to respond. I could see exhaustion overtake his face as he tried to hang in there in order to explain things to me.

"We have to leave now." he said.

"*Leave?* Where are we going, Issa. I have a *job*. *You* have a job. I have a life that I'm trying to get back on track, remember?"

"You won't if we don't leave town now." he said. "New York and Philly are too risky. They're teeming with people we know. We can't even fly safely out of New Jersey."

"Why would we need to *fly* out of anywhere?" I asked with a sense of dread.

Jelaney and Musa looked at Issa and then at me. Baturu looked at me in the rearview mirror and said, "It's okay, Jane you can trust us."

I wasn't so certain of that, especially coming from him. Of all the guys, he was the sketchy-looking one, sporting a tank top, a small collection of beaded bracelets on his arms, a Mohawk, and several tattoos featuring wild animals in the middle of devouring prey.

"Can you gimme some water, Man." Issa asked Jelaney. He turned back to me and said, "We can take you to your mom's place first in Virginia, and rest a while, but then we have to go, all of us."

"Are you kidding me?" I asked.

"We're all connected, Jane." he said. "They know our every relation here. There's nowhere else to hide. We have to leave town, and we have to do it now. I'll tell you the whole story soon."

He drank a little water and climbed across the back seat into the hatch to rest.

***

While Fatou slept and Jelaney and Issa rested in the hatch, I tried to cook up a convincing story for my mom.

"Oh, Ma, why am I showing up on your doorstep with three strange Liberian men, a pregnant woman and my ex live-in boyfriend? Because we're on the run from some more strange Liberian men and, possibly, the police." I muttered to myself in a daze.

"They are not going to the police." Issa moaned from the hatch.

"Shut up, Issa! You don't know shit!" I said.

"You are very angry." he said, rising up to face me.

"Leave me alone!"

"You are mad at me." he went on with a hint of mockery in his voice. "I deserve it."

"Just shut up and go back to sleep, Issa."

"I understand. I understand why you're mad."

"Oh, really? You've suddenly grown a heart?"

"This really had nothing to do with you."

"And suddenly a pair of balls as well!"

"If I had just let you live in your car, this would never have happened to you."

Musa shot me a perplexed glance in the rearview mirror as Issa continued.

"At least they wouldn't have found you so quickly."

"You got that right. That'll teach me to place shelter over autonomy." I said.

"But then we may not have escaped alive, if you hadn't shot that guy."

"So you owe me. Now, will you either tell me what all this is about or shut the hell up?" I had turned to face him but jerked back around when I realized something.

"Oh my God! Goldie's back there!"

Hadn't I lost enough? I didn't want to lose my trusty automobile too!

"No it's not." Baturu assured me. "We have your belongings."

I shook my head in confusion.

"You still haven't explained anything? WHAT IS GOING ON?" I insisted.

My panicked tone must have hit an empathetic nerve, because they gave in and explained.

"We're driving to Atlanta." Musa said. "Baturu knows a guy down there who will take care of us, missing passports and all. I *told* Issa that trouble was brewing and that he needed to prepare these things, but he was apparently… preoccupied. From Atlanta, we need to go to Monrovia and eradicate this problem at the root."

I went off.

"I am not going ANYWHERE with you people! LIBERIA? ARE YOU KIDDING ME? I'm not even a part of all of this. Let me out. Put me out of the car right now!"

"You are a part of this, Jane." Issa went on.

"How?" I asked.

"They don't know which one of you is pregnant. I'm sorry that I didn't make that known, but I couldn't let them kill her. Who knows what they would have done."

I looked at Fatou who was staring at Issa with tears in her eyes.

He went on. "Those guys just got here several hours ago. They been all around Woodland Avenue getting some word on the street about us, and they found me. My brothers warned me about the possibility, but I didn't expect this so soon."

"He was too busy being a playboy." Musa added from the front seat.

Issa rolled his eyes. "We've been hearing through the grapevine about them for years. Anyway, they know that somebody's pregnant and that somebody works with me at the bank. That would be you, Jane. They didn't kill anybody yet, because they didn't know which one of you works at the bank."

"What does my job have to do with any of this?"

"Deana has just accepted a job with the African Development Bank in Liberia. She will be assisting with the securing of land for several redevelopment projects, but she previously did consulting work for several Liberian banks, including our family's. That was how the opportunity with AfDB opened up, as a favor. Her files contain critical information regarding our assets and inheritances."

"I haven't seen any files that have anything to do with her work in Liberia or your family!"

"It doesn't matter." Issa said. "You are her assistant and my girlfriend. They think you have a skeleton key. They're afraid that if they capture us but leave you out there, you could take measures to keep them from the money."

He waited for me to respond while I shook my head, not knowing what to think.

"*Ex*-girlfriend." I corrected him. "Issa, you mean to tell me all you jokers are rolling in dough and you've been living in a hovel eating bread and water since college?"

"I am a simple man." he said stoically.

"You're simple alright." I responded. "Who are these people who want your money?"

Musa interrupted, "Have you at least told her about our parents? You should start there. Please pardon him, Jane, but our difficult family story and our country's history are things that we don't usually discuss openly with others."

I was offended by how much of an "other" Issa considered me to be. But I nodded and tried to wipe the look of contempt off my face, hoping that would encourage him to finally disclose fully.

"You know that they died...during the war... Mom died of a heart attack. It was shortly after dad died. I told you that."

"Um hmm." I said. I always knew there was probably much more to that extremely short story, something heart-wrenching and even heinous. But Issa and I were never confidants. If he didn't want to talk about it, I let him have his space. It's not like I would have been able to coax anything out of him. The man was a vault.

"Our mom attended university in Nigeria where she met our dad. They got married shortly after graduating and started having babies. Mom wanted them to move to her hometown in Liberia, because she figured there would be less competition and greater opportunity for them to enter the banking industry. She was also a bit headstrong and didn't always gel with his very Evangelical family. Mom was very intelligent and had a lot of business sense. She was a competent accountant and was a progressive thinker, pretty moderate on religion in general.

"They moved back to Nigeria briefly, right after I was born, cause some guys they knew in college wanted their help starting another bank. Back then, mom wasn't getting along too well with her mom and her aunts, because they too had converted from Islam to Christianity and criticized her for still identifying as Muslim, for making prayers five times a day and fasting during Ramadan. She missed her family, but she also wasn't eager to deal with them pressuring her to convert.

"But the war changed everything. Mom needed to be closer to her family again, and they needed to be in Liberia to tend to their business. Lots of Nigerians were moving to Liberia at that time, too. Nigeria was one of the first countries to come to Liberia's aid after the war broke out. Business people came to help stabilize the economy and others came with the military peace-keeping forces. Dad worked as a banker. Jelaney's Dad, Uncle Chike, was a soldier with the ECOMOG intervention."

"What's ECOMOG?" I asked.

Baturu said, "The Economic Community Cease-Fire Monitoring Group. It was a conglomerate of West African armed forces, primarily supported by Nigeria."

Issa went on. "Many people saw, and still to this day see, the Nigerians as a boon to the country during that time and in the aftermath of the war. But, there were some guys who didn't want them butting in. Charles Taylor's so-called rebels were their enemies because Taylor was the one who had staged the coup that ousted the previous government and started the conflict in the first place.

"Uncle Chike participated in the 1992 ECOMOG raid and bombing of a Firestone plantation in Harbel. They claimed Taylor's guys were storing some weapons there. A lot of civilians got hurt or died.

"One of Taylor's guys found out about the raid before it happened, and he tried to make a deal with Uncle Chike. He wanted Uncle Chike to arrange a safe, all-expense-paid trip off the plantation and out of the country for a bunch of his family members who lived there. The guy was only fourteen at the time, so I guess he was able to make Uncle Chike feel sorry for him. He had a mom, sister, cousins, uncles— all living there or working for Firestone. In exchange, that guy promised not to get word back to his comrades about the raid.

"Uncle Chike agreed to help at first, but he probably knew the guy would report the plans anyway to get some accolades with his higher ups or something. Uncle Chike went back on his promise after some of his own guys with ECOMOG figured out what he was trying to do. They convinced him to go and kill that rebel guy. They shot him and dumped him on the outskirts of the plantation. His entire family died in the raid."

"Only *he* wasn't dead." Musa added.

"See," Issa continued, "another layer to this whole thing is that, while our fathers were Nigerian, our mothers were Mandinka." He paused and stared into my eyes, like he was making sure I was still paying attention. "Neither group is liked by some Liberians. Mandinkas— or Mandingoes— are considered by some to not be true Liberians."

"Here he goes." Jelaney said with a sigh. "Little history lesson."

"It is *your* heritage." Issa said to him. Fatou sucked her teeth at Jelaney in agreement with Issa's reprimand, but Jelaney just mumbled something under his breath about being "sick and tired of all this factional b.s."

"Mandinkas established one of the greatest empires of West Africa— the Malian Empire. This includes the intellectual and commercial powerhouse, Timbuktu. They got into a lot of shit with the Americo-Liberians who settled the country— those are your people. Actually, everybody who was already there had problems with your people. Unfortunately, the Americos made the mistake of taking the same elitist, colonialist mindset which had oppressed them in America and transporting it to Liberia. It was divide and conquer at its best, executed through the freed slaves who established the nation.

"Anyway, Mandinkas didn't mix well because of their culture and dedication to Islam." Fatou added. "Not only that, but during the war, we were generally peaceful. Mandinkas were terribly persecuted and butchered by the rebels because of that. Charles Taylor said he intended for the war to be a guerilla war, a rebellion led by the citizens themselves. They resented that we wouldn't rebel, and they saw us as an impediment to their efforts."

"So then," I interrupted, "the guy who tried to make a deal with your uncle, he was on the side of guys who didn't like Nigerians or Mandinkas, because they were considered, like, outsiders who weren't necessarily down for the cause?"

"Essentially." Issa said.

"And you all are both Nigerian and Mandinka."

"Yep." Jelaney said, staring out the window.

"Except Fatou," Issa explained. "She's part Mandinka and part Americo."

I was momentarily fascinated by the fact that Fatou, this woman who I considered nothing other than wholly African, was actually a descendent of enslaved black Americans.

"Well, what about the Americos?" I asked. "They were outsiders, too. Since they created so much division with their elitist mentality, were they targeted during the war?"

"Yes!" Issa explained. "But they were the ruling elite, and in the beginning, they had Daddy U.S.A. on their side. Charles Taylor himself is part Americo and part native. I told you he came to power by way of a coup, right? Well he overthrew Samuel Doe, who was the first indigenous head of state in Liberia's history. Samuel Doe overthrew William Tolbert in a coup before that. All these guys had their own ideas of what Liberia should be and who should be cleansed out. Taylor claims he wanted to be a unifier between Americos and natives."

"Why not unify everybody?" I asked.

"That's a whole lot easier said than done." Fatou said.

"Tribalist *bullshit!*" Jelaney shouted. Then he just kept looking out the window, shaking his head as we talked.

Issa continued, "Taylor had some strong Pan-African ideals. Despite his heritage he was very much against western imperial influence— unless it came in the form of funding for his cause, which it supposedly did. His guys trained with Libya's leader, Muammar Qaddafi, who supported so-called liberation movements throughout sub-Saharan Africa for years. But unfortunately, like many *liberators,* it seems that somewhere along the way Taylor became much more interested in power than in freedom. He ran roughshod over anybody who didn't agree with him."

"You say that like he had some good intentions that went bad." Fatou said indignantly. "He just saw an opportunity to grab power, and he did it. He didn't *run roughshod.* He raped, pillaged, and desecrated opposition in Liberia *and* Salone. They used child soldiers. They used women and children as human shields when surrounded by ECOMOG forces. They committed mass amputations. The soldiers violated women and pulled their eyes out so that they could not identify them later. They paraded through streets eating the hearts of their victims. They went around cutting babies out of women's bellies. Those were Taylor's *liberators!*"

"And those are the guys after you." I said with the gravity of the situation sinking in.

"Those are they guys after *us.*" Issa said. "That rebel guy recovered after the plantation bombing and came back looking for Uncle Chike. That's how my dad and Uncle Chike got killed. All of us kids had already left the country during the persecutions.

"Those thugs kept busy waging war until years later. Now they have some free time to hunt us down and squeeze some money out of us. We have the money, but you and Fatou they would have killed for fun."

I looked out the window, taking in everything that they told me.

"Who else knows about them coming here?" I asked.

"I don't know. Only us, I assume." Issa said.

"I don't think they gave away much information when they went around town looking for us. Just pretended to be long lost friends." Baturu added. "People would have the cops on them in a heartbeat. Some shady Africans looking for trouble might not make it past the Philly police as easily as they would Liberian authorities."

"Not during the Nutter administration." Issa quipped.

"Would anybody related to Deana's new job know about all this?" I asked.

"I don't know. Why?" Issa responded.

"Because… I got a call in the office today from someone asking for Deana. Actually, he called several times saying that it was urgent, but he wouldn't leave a detailed message. The last time I spoke with him, he called your family by name and told me to be careful with you guys. He said, if I plan to have anything to do with you long term, I should know that your family has some affiliations that will make life difficult."

Baturu burst into laughter, then Musa and Jelaney joined in.

"He can say that again." Issa said with a calm grin.

"Hey, who do you think that was?" Jelaney asked. "You think someone on AfDB's end is looking out?"

"I don't know." Issa said. "It could be Jajah Uche. He is the only person I know of in our network at AfDB who may be corresponding with Deana's department. Let's hope for the best."

"I have his number." I said.

The guys perked up and looked at me.

"But it's in my purse... which is in my car."

They all looked disappointed, then Musa leaned in to whisper something to Baturu. Finally he turned to me and said, "A friend of ours has your car. She'll keep it out of sight. We'll make a really quick call and get the phone number from her."

He dialed the friend's number and waited for pick up.

"Eleanor... Da-me, Musa. Hada day? ...I tryin'... You've gotten it? ... Nah Gabriel's shop! I told you not to take it there! ... Tracy's garage? Okay. Listen, I need a note from her purse."

"It's a small orange piece of paper, a sticky note." I added. "It should say something like *'AfDB for Deana'* and a phone number."

"Hear?" Musa asked Eleanor. He listened then wrote down the number that she gave him. "What's that? ...Okay... Jane, she says your phone keeps ringing. It's somebody named Devi tryin' to reach you... and some guy named Stephen, an attorney."

My good friend, Devi, was one of the first people I thought to call, but I couldn't risk getting her involved. I had previously told Stephen to just call himself an attorney if Issa ever happened to get a hold of my phone when he rang me. But what was the point in caring any longer what Issa might think about Stephen?

"I thought your attorney's name was Mike." Issa said.

"He's *an* attorney... not mine." I said without any further explanation.

Musa finished up on the phone. "Eleanor, n'mind ya... don't worry, I beg-o..."

"Musa," I asked, "can you get Devi's number too? I don't know it by heart."

He agreed.

Everyone got quiet again after Musa hung up with Eleanor. I looked at each of them and waited for someone to speak.

"Aren't you gonna call him?" I asked.

Musa looked at his phone and then set it down on his leg.

"I don't know if we should." he said.

Jelaney asked, "You think they're tracking?"

"I highly doubt they're that sophisticated." Issa said.

"It's not that." Musa said. "What if it's not Jajah? I don't know if I'm ready to hear who might be on the other end."

10

It was nearing 4 a.m. and we were well on our way down Route 13 South. There was no way we'd risk taking I-95 and running into beltway construction or traffic which could add an hour or more to our trip. By the time we crossed the Virginia border we needed to stop for gas.

There were two store options— the Royal Farms on the opposite side of the median or the Dixieland convenience store on our side which displayed a super-sized confederate flag marking the entrance to my beloved home state.

"Is this gonna be a problem?" Baturu asked me.

"I have no idea." I said. "I always avoid it."

Jelaney jumped in and nervously added, "You know, seeing as this country could very soon elect its first black president, and gun sales are on the rise, and this place seems a little remote, maybe we should—"

"Just go across the street, man." Musa said. "We got no time for redneck bullshit or all your petty fears. There's a break in the median right there."

"Uh huh." Baturu said. He had stalled near the entrance to Dixieland and was just staring across the street.

"Baturu," Musa said, "Right over there, man. The bathroom is probably nicer in there anyway."

"Baturu, what are you doing?" Issa asked. "What are you staring at?"

"There are two cop cars over there." Baturu said slowly.

The brothers looked at each other then at the front door of Dixieland. A haggard man in a "Don't Tread on Me" t-shirt stumbled out of it and started eye-balling our truck.

"Aw, shit." Issa said.

"Calm down." Musa advised. "That guy just looks drunk and homeless. He ain't gonna bother us. Let's just get the gas and go."

"I really need to use the bathroom, and I need a snack." Fatou chimed in.

"Me too." I added. "I finally have an appetite."

"Okay," Musa responded, "Issa, if you would kindly escort your ladies to the restroom just in case anyone in there wants to start whistling Dixie."

"The police are leaving that other place." Jelaney said.

"It's alright." Musa was getting annoyed with all the second guessing. "Let's just get this over with and keep movin'."

When we walked into Dixieland, I was relieved to see that the place was nearly empty. A sleepy-looking clerk gave us a nod and allowed us to move about without any attention to speak of. Issa waited just outside the door while each of us used the bathroom, and we returned the favor.

"Okay," he said with a sigh of relief after finishing up. We all bought a load of snacks then walked out.

After settling back into the truck, we saw the two police cars across the street leave Royal Farms, drive a little ways Northbound, then make U-turns into the Southbound lane. They pulled into the Dixieland parking lot just yards away from us while the guys pumped up the tires. I could hear the conversation between Baturu and Musa intensifying.

"Why are you so nervous? Just be cool and they won't sniff anything out." Musa said.

They both got back into the car, but Baturu still looked very bothered.

"You guys need to know something." he finally blurted out.

As if he expected a sordid tale, Musa asked, "What?"

"It's about this vehicle." Baturu tapped the steering wheel nervously with his index fingers while looking at the cop cars.

"Don't you say it." Musa said.

Baturu closed his eyes and kept tapping.

"Baturu," Issa asked, "what is wrong with the truck?"

"It is not mine." Baturu admitted.

"Who's is it, hmm?" Musa was seething with anger.

Baturu hesitated before Issa punched him in the shoulder.

"The car is stolen." Baturu sat still and waited for their reaction.

"BA-TU-RU!" Fatou yelled.

"I had to quickly get a car that could not be recognized as one of ours!"

"You told me you cut ties with those stolen car dealers." Issa said. "What were you thinking?"

"What are *you* thinking?" Baturu screamed. "This is the least of our worries. Have you forgotten that we have a confirmed killer in the backseat?"

"We don't know for sure that he died." Issa gave me a sympathetic glance.

"Oh... he's dead." Musa added. "Eleanor said so. But the police never got any information. Those thugs got out of there too soon."

Baturu turned on the car and pulled out of the station.

"We'll be rid of this car soon enough." Musa said.

"Hmpf." Fatou shot Baturu a hateful glance.

Everyone settled down again and we made our way to my mom's place.

11

"So it all was very last minute and unexpected," I told my mom over bacon and eggs as everyone looked on. "The two interns that our bank originally chose to participate were preparing to leave for Liberia two days ago. Had gotten their shots and everything. But then they just got yanked from the job— something about them being dishonest about their credentials during the interview process."

I looked at Issa and hoped he would say something or at least nod to agree with my absurd story. Then I kept talking.

"Fatou and the guys haven't been back home since they came here nearly a decade ago, so they all decided now would be a great time for them to visit… as a family."

Issa stared at my mouth like he was amazed. He'd never known me to lie until very recently. Finally, he nodded and said,

"Yah."

"Anyway," I went on, "Deana, the attorney I'll be accompanying, is scheduled to fly into Monrovia in a few days. I'll continue as her assistant and Issa will be acting as a liaison between her and a network of bankers there."

I paused to consider whether there was anything else my mom may want to know. I wanted her to ask as few questions as possible.

"It's a really short project." I said. "We'll only be there to support her during the first procurement which could be a month."

Musa scrunched his brow and shook his head quickly, causing me to adjust my estimation.

"Or could be a few weeks."

He coughed and tilted his head as if it were a signal. Getting the timeline wrong could provoke more questions down the line.

"Could be less time than that." I concluded. "It's really up in the air."

"I just wish you could see Terrence before you leave." my mom said. "You all, Jane's brother, Terrence, is in Italy. His job regularly sends him on overseas projects, too. Well, Jane, after everything you've gone through since graduation, this is truly wonderful to see that God has opened a door to such a blessing for you. Traveling overseas again! And this time not runnin' from some crazy fool."

"It's amazing how things work out." I said.

"And I'm happy for you, too, Issa. Jane told me about your layoff. It's good to see you back on your feet." She gave him a loving pat on the shoulder.

"We're not out of the woods yet with this economy, Ms. Yvonne." Issa said. "I'm sure you've seen the news about

Lehman Brothers. They just made the largest bankruptcy filing in U.S. history. They had over six hundred billion in assets. It's just gonna be a domino effect. But so far we've been shielded, largely because Arc One stayed away from subprime lending."

While Issa caught up with Mom, I could see that Fatou was eyeballing them and assessing their interaction. She seemed surprised that he was so familiar with my mom. Even I was surprised that the two of them had established such a genuine connection when she visited me a year earlier. He took to her the way I guessed he would any loving mother figure, and she wanted the best for a young, black man who showed promise.

Next, Mom went around the living room trying to recall everyone's names.

"Is it Musa?" She asked while gently placing her hand on his back.

"Yes ma'am. Like Moses."

"Yep, I remember you saying that." She moved on. "And you're... is it Bantu?"

"Close. It's Baturu." he said with a smile.

"Ba-too-roo. You two are Issa's brothers right. I can see the resemblance.   ...I'm sorry, honey. What's your name again?" She asked Jelaney.

"Jay-lon-ee."

My mom repeated after him then asked, "Are you related to Issa, too?"

"Yes, ma'am, we're cousins."

After him, Mom moved on to Fatou.

"Now I know your name begins with an 'F'."

"It's Fatou, ma'am." she said with a childlike softness in her voice.

"Oh, that's a beautiful name. And are you related to Issa, too?"

"Yes... I am his cousin as well."

I immediately felt horrible. Not only was I lying my behind off to my mother's face for the first time in my life, but I felt like I was driving a wedge between a pregnant woman and her baby's father in the process. I tried to wrap up the conversation with Mom.

"So, I hope our unexpected visit won't get in the way of anything you have to do today. We'll really just be resting up before hitting the road tomorrow."

"Oh, well this is my weekend off. I was planning to go up to Maryland to visit a friend of mine for the weekend. Do you all need anything? There are a few things in there but I didn't get groceries."

"Don't worry about anything, Ma." I assured her. "We'll get everything we need."

***

After Mom changed out of her caftan and into her traveling clothes, she set her suitcase and purse by the front door. She held a large bottle of Extra Virgin Olive Oil in her hand.

"Come here and lemme anoint you." she said pulling me over to the console table by the door.

"Oooo yes!" she exclaimed. "Father God, I come before you right now, giving honor to you for this *wonderful* opportunity that you have blessed Jane and Issa with. Now I ask, Father, that you will place your Spirit of Excellence upon them and help them to carry out their duties to the best of their abilities."

Jelaney had just used the bathroom and stepped into the hallway. He politely bowed his head and put an index finger in the air while walking past us.

"Let this be an opportunity that will lead to more opportunities that will be even more of a blessing to their lives and to others."

She tightened her grip on my now saturated forehead as she continued with the conclusion of her prayer.

"Now, keep every robbing, murderous, mischievous demon, all disease, and anything that would cause them harm away from their path! Preserve them from every temptation that would derail them from the plan you have for their lives."

She almost pushed my head into the wall while emphasizing *"temptation"* and *"derail"*.

"And bring 'em back safe and sound."

I breathed a sigh of relief. My head was again free from the prayer grip, and the support of that prayer took away some of the fear and pressure that I was feeling. I leaned in to give her a goodbye hug. She looked at me with mild suspicion and asked,

"You think I'm not raising my eyebrow about you and these FOUR men you just showed up on my doorstep with?"

"Huh?" I said in shock. "Ma!"

"I see something. I *see* it. You just make sure you stay focused on your work while you're over there. And none o' that shackin' like you did in Bermuda. You said they gon' have ya in a hotel. Stay in *your* room."

"Ma, I understand your concern, but you know I'm pushing thirty, right?"

"Twenty-six ain't pushing thirty, and thirty don't mean you know everything. I don't know which one of 'em ya got your eye on. Could be any one of 'em, except Issa."

She placed her keys on the table and walked back toward the living room.

"You all, if you don't mind, I'd like to say a prayer with you. D-do you all pray?"

Musa answered, "We come from a Muslim background, ma'am. Prayer is not a problem for us. We would appreciate that very much."

She had us huddle and join hands. Then she said one more prayer for all of us, thankfully minus the anointing oil. The moment she was in her car and on her way we reconvened in the living room to figure out our next move.

"First things first— the truck." Musa said to Baturu.

"Yes," Issa said, "we have got to get rid of that thing. Ms. Yvonne is gracious enough to lend us her home. We cannot bring trouble of any kind here."

Fatou sucked her teeth and rolled her eyes at his response.

"How do we get rid it? And how do we get another one?" Jelaney asked.

Musa reached into his back pocket for his wallet.

"I tried to tell you guys to get ready. Let's see how prepared you are. Empty your pockets... Now!"

"I guess that doesn't include me, 'cause I'm most assuredly broke." I mumbled before plopping down on the couch to observe their plan.

"Well, your help has been invaluable so far." Fatou assured me. It was nice to see that Issa was the only target of her wrath.

"Are you serious?" Musa asked before grabbing the wallets one-by-one and frantically emptying the contents. "You jack asses didn't bring cash!"

"I have some cash."

"This is not enough, Baturu!" Musa barked. "Every last one of you has credit and debit cards. What do you think is going to happen when you use any of them? Those accounts have already been compromised!"

Issa explained. "Right after you called I got into all that stuff with Fatou and Jane. That druggie down the hall called the cops and held us up. Then those guys were all over us. I never had a chance to get to a bank."

"Issa... you *work* at a fucking bank! Last night was not the first time we discussed this. Never mind that, now. Here is what we have to do: We go somewhere— today— and get a cheap car to get us to Atlanta. Something that will cost... around twelve hundred. We keep the rest for food and our transport. We leave here as soon as we have that car. We'll take shifts driving so that everybody sleeps. I don't know how the hell we're gonna get six people to Liberia with three missing passports, but we'll have to figure it out when we talk to Baturu's guy."

"Okay, so how do we get rid of the car?" Jelaney asked.

"I say we drown it." Baturu said. "Take it right to one of those inlets. Give me an excuse to see the beach before we head out."

"This is not a holiday, Baturu." Issa snapped. "Can't we torch it in a campground somewhere?"

"Really? That would draw way too much attention." Baturu argued.

"Yeah," I added, "especially with all these people destroying their gas-guzzling SUVs for insurance money."

"Why don't you tap your network of thieves for a local chop shop?" Fatou asked Baturu.

"That might be a good idea if all my contacts weren't in Philly and New York." he retorted. "We can't risk calling there again."

"I know somebody who might be able to help us find one." I said.

Everyone looked in my direction.

"My dad. He probably knows somebody."

"How sure are you of that?" Musa asked me.

"Almost certain." I said. "Hey, it's worth a shot, especially for the extra cash."

Musa got on the phone with the contact in Atlanta, and the guys started looking for cheap cars online while I called my dad. I briefed him on our fictitious assignment in Liberia and explained that we were in route to Atlanta, but that our rickety SUV just wouldn't hold up through the rest of the trip.

"Hey, why not get a little money out of it, right?" my dad agreed. "That'll be my contribution to your trip."

There was no way that I was going to conduct mission impossible overseas without paying him a visit. I told him that I would come over, and he agreed to check into his contacts while Issa and I got on the bus to meet him.

"Just go to your granny's house, instead." he told me. "I gotta cut the grass for her in a lil' bit."

"Uh, okay," I said wondering how well my lying skills would hold up in front of Granny, Queen of Interrogation. I would have to try to make this the sweetest, shortest goodbye-pending-certain-danger ever.

***

"Why ya can't just fly to Georgia? The job won't pay for it?" Granny asked from her recliner.

My dad sat on the porch making hushed phone calls.

"The economy is causing them to tighten the purse strings a bit when it comes to employee travel." I said. "They're giving us a limited stipend, which we'd rather save for other expenses. Plus the road trip is kind of fun. I've never been to Atlanta, so it'll be a cool layover."

"Mm hmm." She moaned with squinty eyes. God love her, she was faithfully suspicious and trying to get the details— every single detail.

"Seem like you oughta be resting 'stead of driving all that way."

"We'll all take turns driving." I assured her.

"What kinda car ya got right now?"

"It's an old Durango."

"I thought they was alright trucks...ain't that what they say?

I hunched my shoulders, not knowing what *"they"* said about any particular truck.

"Ya granddaddy had one. It was a good truck. It ain't *your* truck?"

"No, granny, I still have my Cavalier."

"I know. Broke a you is I know you didn't go and buy no truck. What's wrong with the truck?"

"It's old, granny." I sighed with exasperation. "Just old... too many things wrong with it to count."

"Whoever had it didn't take care of it." She added indignantly. She and her late husband had not been ones to neglect properly maintaining their belongings.

"I guess so."

"*Who* ya workin fuh?"

"Deana Bell, she's the attorney who's traveling there."

Issa gave me a wide-eyed look to let me know I was treading into dangerous territory by giving away names.

"How long ya stayin' over there?"

"A few weeks."

"Why they gon' send ya'll to *Liberian*, after all that war and mess over there? They couldn't send ya nowhere peaceful?"

"Liberia, Granny. That's where the help is needed, and since I'm working for an attorney who—"

"Who else ya say goin' with ya?" she butted in.

"Issa's brothers and two other family members."

"Bunch of men?"

"And one other woman, Granny. We'll be sleeping in different places."

"And what's the name of the bank?"

Issa jumped in to help, since the speed at which she was hurling questions was clearly beginning to overwhelm me.

"Ma'am, Liberia is our home country, so I can assure you Jane won't have to navigate it without lots of help."

She looked away from him and toward the TV with a stubborn look of concern on her face.

"Yeah... but all that killin' and mayhemin' going on over there, ya'll don't need to be going to them kinda parts of the world. Don't need to take no assignment like that. Take another job... and, what's wrong with the car ya got?" she looked over Issa's head and back at me.

I knew she knew that she had already asked that question— twice. The answer simply not been thorough enough for her.

"It's a piece of junk, Granny." I replied. "Needs expensive repairs and we'd rather just scrap it for cash."

"You would think a bank would give ya'll a better send off than that." She started rocking back and forth in her recliner and fixed her mouth for another question, but my dad walked in and got her attention.

"Miles, what ya doin' out there on the phone and ya daughter sitting here getting ready to go to Africa? Who was on the phone?"

"Celia, watch the stories and mind ya business! I gotta make one mo' phone call, Jane. I just need to get something from upstairs."

"What ya gotta get from up there?" Granny asked.

While Miles ran upstairs, ignoring her question, she decided to go in the kitchen and start dinner.

"Well, I'ma go in here and clean these turkey wings."

Issa waited until she was out of sight and joked, "I guess I'm a professional liar now, hanging out with you."

I looked at him surprised. "You were a pro long before today."

"You just don't understand." he said.

"Nothing *to* understand." I responded.

"Then again," he said, "maybe you do."

He tried to command my attention with a stare, but I chose to keep looking ahead at the TV. Then we both heard someone coming down the stairs.

I looked up expecting it to be Miles. Instead, the person stopped just short of the wall which divided the family room from the stairway. Suddenly, my uncle Jean's slender, bald head peeked around the corner of the wall. After seeing us, he quickly pulled it back.

Issa looked at me confused. I tapped my finger on my thigh wondering how long it would take my uncle Jean to come down the last three steps with a stranger in the house. I also wondered how much of the weirdness in my family could possibly be revealed in the short amount of time that we were there. But then, there was certainly no need to feel embarrassed considering Issa's family drama.

"How you doing, Jean." I said, like I always did despite his reclusive tendencies. A few seconds later he revealed himself, came down those last three steps, gave us both a quick wave without looking in our direction, and went into the kitchen to make his lunch.

"He's the family hermit." I said to Issa. "Don't ask."

Miles came back down and quietly handed me the address to the chop shop.

"Uh, I didn't have any luck getting a hold of anybody, Jane. If you keep at it, you might be able to get somebody on the phone before too late. Ya'll want me to give you a ride back to your mom's house?" he asked.

Normally I wouldn't have said yes. Miles and I both knew the protocol— since their divorce, Mom did not want him to have her phone number or address. But he wanted to help us in any way he could, and we were pressed for time.

"Actually, that would be a big help. Thanks." I said.

"I'll just drop you in the neighborhood. You ain't gotta tell me what house she stay in."

When we got near my mom's place, we saw Baturu and Musa stepping out of an old Ford Explorer which was parked right next to the Durango that we drove down in. Issa introduced them to Miles and they all shook hands and exchanged friendly small talk.

I was grateful that Miles had just helped us out. I was also happy to see that he was happy and at a good place in his life since returning from rehab. He was managing to hold down a job while maintaining a car and an apartment across the street from Granny. I hoped he would keep it up, since he had struggled with relapses many times before.

For a moment I observed the way that he stood there talking with the guys, as if there was an unspoken familiarity between them. I could tell he liked Issa. This was the first time Miles had met anyone that I was dating. Too bad Issa was all wrong for me.

The guys walked to my mom's place while I wrapped up with Miles.

"Back to the motherland!" he said with joy.

"Yeah, this won't be like Tanzania, though. Lot of hard work this time."

"Ah, you'll be alright. You get this project done and who knows where they might send you next. That's what they got Terrence doing on his job—travelin' the world."

I nodded.

"I'm proud of you." he said, reaching out for a hug.

After a quick pat on the back, I looked into his eyes and hoped that he didn't see the trouble in mine. I wanted to tell him what was going on. I knew he would have an objective enough perspective to offer real help without getting overly emotional. I wanted to relieve the burden of the secret, to not feel so alone in this.

But I wasn't sure how to communicate something so heavy and full of emotions to him, and I simply couldn't risk bringing anyone else into this mess, especially the people that I cared about most. I silently waved goodbye as he drove off then went back inside to prepare for our trip to Atlanta.

***

Later that evening as we all stood waiting for Baturu to shift the Durango into neutral and release it into North Bay, Jelaney asked,

"Are you sure this is our best dumping option? There seemed to be a lot of houses not very far away. I feel like some vacationer is gonna cruise up here any minute and catch us."

"The coast here is lined with military bases, resorts and neighborhoods." I said. "A semi-secluded place like this is best."

"Yeah," Musa said, "and since we don't have a whole lot of time to consider other options, let's just get it over with. Business must be booming at that chop shop if they couldn't even answer the phone."

As the roof of the Durango disappeared into the bay, Issa whispered to me, "Too bad we couldn't stay longer."

"Yeah, well, I have you to thank for that." I said.

"Might have given us some time to make up. Virginia *is* for lovers."

I looked over at Fatou, who was nodding off in the Explorer, then back at Issa.

"That supposed to be a joke?" I asked. "You might wanna stop while you're ahead, or that Durango may not be the only dead weight lying in a bay tonight."

12

Baturu's friend, Salim, was a doctor who had spent time overseas treating the injured in the wakes of conflicts and natural disasters. He had helped several people gain asylum and access to medical care in America. He was also quite familiar with the unconventional means employed by some to get in and out of the country without proper documentation.

We all sat around his sprawling living room watching the national news and marveling over the fact that the U.S. could very well be electing its first African American president in less than two months.

"I can't believe that our future children will likely be born into the era of the first black American president." Issa remarked in awe.

Fatou and I acted as though we didn't hear him.

Despite his enthusiasm, his words faded into a low mumble. "For the first phase of their lives... that will be all they know." He had a very intriguing point, but likely realized that he should probably not wax sentimental about expecting a child in the presence of both his side chick and the girlfriend that he had knocked up while temporarily harboring said side chick in his home.

"That will be a challenge, traveling while pregnant." Salim said to Fatou. "The conditions of this trip are certainly not ideal."

He looked around the room at all of us and continued. "Listen, about your travel arrangements, you won't have much trouble getting out of the U.S. The biggest problem will be getting back in. Now you *could* just hop on a plane from here without an immigration check on this end. But that will leave a paper trail. Those guys have connections, and they will be expecting you when you arrive in Liberia. I know you need to buy yourself some time to plan and scope things out once you get there. So..."

"What?" Musa asked. "What other options do we have?"

"I previously explored one option. I know a guy who could sneak you onto a barge... in an ocean container."

"Is this guy crazy?" Musa asked Baturu.

Salim went on, "But I understand that, with a pregnant woman in tow, that would not be ideal. Is it absolutely necessary for her to go? Is there no one she can stay with?"

I wanted to hear the answer, because I was still looking for some loophole that would give me a good reason to sit out this excursion, too.

"If any of us stay, it's only gonna be a matter of time before we're found." Issa said. "We can't risk leaving anybody behind, and we won't split up, if that's what you're thinking."

"Traveling by barge wouldn't be ideal for anybody." Baturu said in disbelief.

"Friggin' reverse middle passage?" Musa added. "No way."

"Well then, you'll have to fly," Salim concluded. "but not commercially... which is good, because you can fly straight and not have to connect in Europe or anywhere else."

We all looked at each other as if unsure. The idea of avoiding any possible airport snags was appealing, but we had no idea what we would be exchanging our safe, predictable flight for.

"Who would we be flying with?" Baturu asked.

"I got you covered!" Salim said abruptly before picking up his phone and calling someone.

"Yeah, man!" he said. "They're gonna go with the private flight."

He hung up the phone and smiled at Baturu.

"You are on your way! Why don't you get comfortable in some of my guest rooms. Dinner will be ready soon. Then you can all get some rest before your early flight."

And just like that, the next leg of our journey was nearly underway.

***

I stood in the kitchen pushing the scraps from my plate into the trash, and I could see Issa approaching from the corner of my eye. Fatou and I still had not gotten thoroughly acquainted, but I could feel a deliberate, unspoken peace between us.

Ultimately, I wasn't the kind of woman to blame another woman for her partner's dishonesty, and she seemed to see things the same way. Actually, I had been fantasizing about the many ways in which I might seriously injure Issa, and I got the sense that she may have shared that fantasy as well.

She sat eating at the kitchen island, and neither of us said a word. Issa glanced at Fatou then up at me with a smirk.

"I am impressed by how well you two are tolerating each other." he said.

"Why would we have a problem tolerating each other?" Fatou snapped back. "You're the lying sac of shit."

"Hey, why don't we just give the thugs what they want and hand over Issa?" I asked Fatou. "He alone could lead them to the money."

"Yeah, let them hold *him* for ransom." She agreed. "And if they decide to kill him anyway... meh."

"Ladies, don't you think you're being a little extreme?" Jelaney asked while digging into the fridge for a beer. "You'd hand him over to a Liberian rebel death squad out of spite?"

Issa grabbed the beer from Jelaney and said, "It's Ramadan."

"Okay." Jelaney said as he grabbed the beer back and turned around to open it. "You're devout all of a sudden? Must be a very recent development. How pregnant is she?"

"You know I never drink. And we need to be disciplined in our thinking right now." Issa said in a sudden bout of seriousness. "You lack moderation. And I, for one, am looking for any help we can get."

"You're about as believable as Aunt Nyima, dragging out that kimar and dusting it off once a year for Ramadan only to put it back in time for Christmas."

Uh oh. I expected Issa to take that comment as a jab against his beloved, deceased mother. Instead, he loosened up again and joked around with Jelaney, lightening the mood.

"Hey, she was a smart, frugal woman, and you can't beat free stuff— no matter what holiday brings it."

While they shared memories, I walked out of the kitchen and upstairs toward the room that Fatou and I would be sharing for the night. As pretentious as Issa may have seemed in his renewed piety, his comments certainly inspired me to turn in early so that I could send up a prayer of my own.

Before getting to the bedroom, though, I remembered that I wanted to talk to Issa about exactly why it was that the thugs believed I had a "skeleton key" to Deana's files. At the last minute, I was still trying to figure out a way to weasel out of this debacle.

"Issa!" I yelled from the upstairs hallway.

I thought I faintly heard someone answer "What?" but I wasn't sure.

"Issa!" I yelled again.

"What?" Musa said, peeking out from inside the bedroom two doors down the hall.

"Oh no, I'm sorry, Musa. I was calling Issa." I leaned over the railing to see if I could spot Issa anywhere.

"You sure?" Musa asked me.

"Uh, yeah, I was calling Issa."

"Really? You weren't calling me at all?" he asked with a smile and a hint of exaggerated disappointment.

"Um, no." I said with a chuckle.

Finally, Issa came walking around the corner from the dining room and said, "What is it?"

As Issa made his way up the stairs, Musa said, "I wouldn't mind if you were." then went back into his room.

"You called me?" Issa asked. There was a look of resignation on his face as if he expected another verbal beating, but my mind was lingering on Musa's flirting.

"What are you smiling about?" Issa asked.

I inadvertently tilted my head in the direction of Musa's room then tried to change my expression and ask the question about Deana's files.

"What are you doing up here?" he abruptly asked me.

"*Excuse* me?" I asked, amazed that he would have the nerve to question my behavior.

While Jelaney and Baturu walked up the stairs and bypassed him on the way their rooms, he folded his arms and looked back at me like a parent waiting for a rebellious child's apology.

"Good night, guys." I said in the sweetest tone that I could muster. "I'm sure everything will work out tomorrow."

"What are you up to?" he asked once they were in their rooms.

"Preparing for bed, but I figured everyone could use a little encouragement to boost their spirits. Nothing wrong with an encouraging word."

"Get your mind right, girl." he said as if his words could shame me.

"You know, the chance to meet your brothers just might have made this whole mess at least halfway worth my while. Baturu is such a gentleman."

"Jane!"

"And Musa has a wonderful smile. And tall. And he really has a leader's way about him. You could learn a thing or two from that one."

"Why don't you go in there and text your booty caller. Oh that's right, too bad you don't have your phone. You must be getting bored."

"Booty caller? You are clueless! Why don't you go downstairs and act like you give a crap about your baby mama before she slips into a depression or goes nuts and tries to smother you in your sleep!"

"That would make *two* crazy killers!" he shouted before storming back downstairs.

I didn't wait another second before slamming my bedroom door. I took a nice hot shower and attempted to relax in the well-appointed room that Salim had prepared for us. Not long after I bedded down, Fatou followed suit.

"If you don't mind my asking, how are you feeling?" I asked.

"Oh, girl, you don't have to tread lightly with me. We're in this mess together. Honestly, I feel okay. I've only been having nausea in the evenings just before dinner. It's always the smell of the meat cooking, but some ginger beer helps."

"But aren't you afraid? Running around like this, being on the run for your life. I couldn't imagine doing this knowing that I was carrying a child."

"I know, but... I really don't have any other choice... and I trust them. They're my family. Even Issa, at least in this situation."

I got the sense that she really did feel safe with the guys, but that she also had to believe that their plan would work. I didn't want to cause her any stress by doubting it.

"So, what do you do back in Philly?" I asked. "Did you go to school there, too?"

"I manage a daycare in Colwyn." She answered. "I honestly thought getting a degree in education would help me avoid the financial services industry. My dad was an insurance broker. I thought they'd have no excuse to try to drag me into their drama if my career had nothing to do with money. So much for that."

"You actually chose a career with that in mind?"

"Not necessarily. I enjoy what I do, and I thought being an outsider would have some advantages."

"You've been involved with Issa for a while, huh?"

"We've all stuck together since back home, basically. Our families were close, and when I came here they helped me transition. Issa and I dated since high school."

"Wow." I said. "It's amazing how someone can have a whole other life right under your nose and you don't know it."

"Or choose not to see it." Fatou said. "...I knew there was something weird about that stupid TRESemmé shampoo...and that stuffed monkey under the bed!"

***

Early the next morning, the sound of Salim's prayer broadcast woke us up. It was piping through a hardwired audio system throughout the entire house. We all got dressed then met him at the entry circle out front.

We didn't have to wait long for a dark blue minivan to come speeding up next to us. Salim flung open the sliding door and said,

"I will not be accompanying you to the airstrip. The less of us there, the better. You will take off before sunrise and land in beautiful Liberia before you know it."

"You still haven't told us much." Musa said. "Is there anything else we should know or be prepared for?"

"My people, I tell you, everything is taken care of." Salim assured him. "Just get there, safely handle your business, and get back here to continue your life. Kul 'am wa enta bi-khair! May *every* year find you in good health, all of you!"

He shoved some vitamins into Fatou's jacket pocket then vigorously shook our hands before sending us off. About twenty minutes later, the mysterious van pulled onto a secluded airstrip. The driver turned around and, quite unceremoniously, gestured for us to exit the van. He then got out and silently directed us to an impressive, blue and white Cessna, like the ones wealthy CEO's use for business travel. The sight of it would have given me some solace if it wasn't for the strange behavior of our driver.

"Which airstrip is this?" Musa asked him.

The driver only furrowed his brow, put his finger over his lips and shook his head.

Once we were all seated on the plane, our driver gestured for us to fasten our seatbelts. He quickly ran up to the cockpit then came back with a backpack. He reached in, pulled out some tangled up oxygen masks, and handed one to each of us.

"What do these even connect to?" Fatou asked while looking at the ceiling for the oxygen supply."

Without any instruction from our driver, we each found our corresponding oxygen sources and noted their locations as he disappeared into the cockpit. He emerged again with a huge canvas bag and set it down on the floor.

Silently, he lifted one motorcycle helmet from the bag and handed it to Baturu.

"What?" I said quietly. We all looked at each other confused.

The driver quickly waved his hand toward the rest of us, directing Baturu to pass the helmet down as he pulled the second, third, and all other helmets from the bag.

"You have gotta be kidding me. I'm not putting this thing on." I set the helmet on the floor in front of my seat in disbelief.

Musa lowered the helmet to his lap and asked the driver, "Ay, man. This is confusing. What's with the helmets?"

The driver looked back at him calmly and shrugged his shoulders before quickly exiting the plane.

"What the hell are we doin'?" Musa said, sinking into his seat.

"Helmets? Really? Is our pilot that much of an amateur?" Fatou asked.

"How the heck is this thing supposed to make it across the Atlantic?" I asked, nearly in a panic. "I mean, it's sexy, but can it even hold enough fuel for that? How long is this flight gonna take? Baturu?!"

Everybody looked at him.

"How did your friend Salim arrange this mess, anyway?" I asked. "Our driver's mute! Doesn't tell us anything about what's going on! We aren't riding Harley's to Liberia! This is supposed to be a safe, private flight. Even if we do crash, these helmets aren't gonna do a thing for us! It's crazy!"

"She is absolutely right." Fatou said with her index finger in the air. "This does not at all feel like a safe situation."

Jelaney sat strapped into his seat with his helmet on and his arms folded tightly across his chest. He just shook his head as all of our faith in this method of transport crumbled.

"Man, where's the pilot." Musa asked. "Maybe he can give us some details to put minds at ease."

"Yeah, I'm not getting the sense that this is gonna be as simple as Salim made it out to be." Baturu said as he stood to follow Musa.

"It's gonna *feel* like riding in a tumble dryer, that's for damn sure." Issa said, still seated and only appearing mildly annoyed.

"No. No. *No!*" I said while unclicking my seatbelt and heading back toward the door.

As Issa and Musa lunged forward to keep me from grabbing the latch, the pilot appeared.

"I understand your concerns!" he yelled over us with hands raised in the air. He was smiling from ear to ear.

"Please, I understand your trepidation. But I can assure you that I and this machine will provide you with safe, efficient travel. You won't, however, be provided with a meal, so I hope you brought snacks." He chuckled lightly.

"I certainly have an appetite." Issa said sarcastically.

"I'm sorry," the pilot continued. "The helmets were a little joke which I thought might break the ice...your driver was a bit drab. The joke was lost in translation."

He attempted to laugh again as we all stared blankly back at him.

"I'm transporting them along with the plane. Anyway, I am Sebastian Ejiofor. I am an accomplished pilot with over fifteen years of ferry flying experience."

"Ferry flying?" I asked.

"Yes, after purchase, those for whom the cost of shipping a plane to their destination would be prohibitive choose to simply have their planes flown to them. I do the flying— the ferrying."

"You are absolutely certain that this small plane can make it across the Atlantic?" Fatou asked.

"Definitely! The owner had an auxiliary fuel tanked installed recently just for that assurance. Would you like to see the installation photos? I took them while monitoring the process on behalf of the owner, a friend of mine."

He carefully pulled out his phone and extended his hand for us to gather around for a look.

"Hey, is that an LG Renoir?" Baturu asked.

"Yes! The world's first full touchscreen camera phone. It was just released. I only use the best tools and technology."

Baturu nodded with enthusiasm and went to his seat.

"Well he may be impressed," Fatou said, "but there are still some things we'd like to know."

"Okay." Sebastian said.

"Well, how long is this flight supposed to take?" I asked.

"It's roughly a four hour flight." he said.

"Oh, that's all?" I asked, surprised and relieved.

"Can we see your credentials?" Musa asked. Issa stood by nodding.

Sebastian immediately furnished his Airline Transport Pilot Certificate and airport and customs security badges.

"How much turbulence are you expecting for this flight?" Musa asked while looking at Jelaney, who was still seated with his helmet on. Baturu knocked on it to get Jelaney's attention then told him to take it off.

"Only a few bumps at take-off and landing. I must tell you that it is currently the rainy season in Liberia, but the weather looks okay for now. It should be a pretty smooth flight. This is a Cessna Citation, folks, a sky limo! Relax and *enjoy* it. It's not every day that you'll have a chance to take a joy ride in one of these babies."

Sebastian walked around checking everyone's seatbelts as we strapped in with calmer nerves. Before he returned to the cockpit and prepared for takeoff, Musa asked him one more question.

"What happens when we get there?"

"Quiet arrival. This is a private aircraft simply being delivered to its owner, with a supply stop in Liberia on the way to Nigeria. We land in Harper, Maryland County. You have people there, yes?"

Musa nodded.

"That is all you need to know." Sebastian said.

Musa turned to Issa and explained, "Good, we're not flying into Monrovia. Even if they have any idea that we're returning, they probably won't be expecting us at Tubman Airport or anywhere in Maryland. That should get us a little time."

"Yeah," Issa said, "Aunt Edna and Aunt Caroline have been away from the family for a while. Hopefully those guys know nothing about them. They will be more than happy to see us. Fatou should have a safe place to stay with them while we take care of things."

"Will *I* be safe with Aunt Edna and Caroline too?" I asked. "I don't know what we're doing!"

"Jane, please, we're gonna need your help in Monrovia." Issa said. "Will you just relax for the time being and we'll discuss everything when we get to Harper? We'll have more help there."

Musa gave me a reassuring glance and said, "We promise, we will have a solid plan for Monrovia. There's no need to worry."

"Yeah, okay." I barely believed them, but since I hadn't figured out a way to avoid globetrotting with these guys, I had to settle for the uncertainty.

We floated into the clouds with nothing but an immeasurable expanse of inhospitable sea beneath us. Bright orange rays flooded the cabin and ricocheted off the luscious, cream leather seats, causing us to squint and turn away. The sight seemed nearly as intense as the heat of the very sun which created it, and about as violent as the dangers ahead.

"Here you go again, Jane." I thought. *"Let's hope you don't completely melt this time."*

For the first time in my life, the sight of the sunrise was not at all beautiful. I hated it. I craved the cover of night. And yet there was nowhere else to fly except eastward, right into the direction of that hot, blazing sun.

Part 2

In the shadow of death

the brave ignite life.

13

Landing on African soil again felt, oddly, cathartic. It was as if that same gorgeous hinterland that I had explored several years before in Tanzania, was greeting me again in Liberia. Though this land had been stained with far too much blood, the beaches of Cape Palmas still seemed unspoiled— maybe due to the cleansing power of the waters.

I remembered how beautiful the sight of un-manicured trees and lawns could be, how raw, and unbothered, seemingly touched by nothing except the rains and morning dew. The water and the plentiful green were permanent harbingers of life and life renewed, no matter what.

Our cabs left the main roads and snaked through a twisted array of orange dirt streets and flooded, gut-jolting pot holes. I usually had a pretty good sense of direction, but it was tested on this disorienting and unfamiliar ride.

We passed countless homes with stained mud brick walls and tin roofs, fronted by small vegetable gardens, livestock, and random people carrying on with their day. We eventually left those behind and rode for several minutes without seeing anything but greenery.

Just before reaching the Atlantic shore, we approached an interesting house. It was reminiscent of some hobbit cottage, but with a decidedly African aesthetic. It had little pots of pepper plants hanging from the roof with their countless buds creating a red and green show reminiscent of Christmas. There were numerous pineapple plants looking like gigantic spiders sitting around the yard. Palm trees surrounded the property.

The house was at least three times as large as most of the ones we'd seen along the way. It was actually made up of several different brick box structures, each one elevated above the ground at a slightly different height and joined together by short stairways and arched, outdoor vestibules. The walls were well tended and painted teal with little pictures of playing children splashed all over them in shades of white and yellow. The roof was thatch.

We saw Aunt Edna, standing next to the main house, waiting for a bucket underneath a rainwater collector to fill up. She carefully placed the bucket on her head and approached us slowly. All the guys stood still and waited for her. They had hopeful looks on their faces but stood like statues in anticipation of her reaction.

After taking a long look at the guys, she stopped several yards away from us, removed the bucket from her head and put on her glasses. She continued squinting and looking them over as if thinking long and hard. Then she stretched out her hand toward the house and, in a deep and raspy voice, said,

"Here, we built this for you. Come in!"

Immediately after we all walked into the house, Aunt Caroline dropped a clay bowl that she was holding. It shattered into shards as she ran toward the guys and fell into a kneel crying. Aunt Edna stood by nodding with an ear to ear smile and gave each of them a long hug.

When the Aunts were done hugging them, they both sniffled, hugged each other and started hugging the guys all over again. Each time one of them tried to speak, she would break into sobs and resign to just cry.

There was too much emotion in the air for the men to remain untouched. One by one they succumbed to the waves of fear, sorrow, and the joy of their reunion. I thought that I should look away, but I couldn't when tears welled up in Issa's eyes. He tried gently pulling away from Aunt Edna, but when she embraced him again, he quietly closed his eyes, relaxed his shoulders and remained still.

I was afraid my presence would embarrass them or dampen the moment or something, so I quietly walked back out to the porch where I didn't even realize Fatou had been sitting all along.

"Was that rude of me to go in there like that?" I asked her.

"No." she said. "Guess we should just give them some time though, yeah?"

"Yeah."

It was quiet all around us except for the pattering rain and some intermittent sniffles and sobs from inside the house.

"What do you know about their Aunts?" I asked Fatou. "Why were they apart from the rest of the family for so long?"

"They're from Issa's mom's side of the family. They're sisters of the boys' grandmother. Back in the day, they, along with a whole group of women, made friends with some Episcopalians. The aunties eventually converted to Christianity and moved out here to teach at an orphanage before the war.

"You know from what Issa told you that their mom sort of had a mind of her own. When *her* mother converted to Christianity, she didn't. She had her own misgivings even about Islam and had some pretty moderate religious leanings in general, even though she couldn't always express them openly. It caused a bit of a rift. Then later, because of the dads' business dealings and the enemies they acquired, it was too dangerous for the aunties to have much contact with them."

"Girls, come!"

We turned to see both aunts standing in the doorway. Aunt Edna began rubbing my belly and said, "Our family is being restored!"

"Uh, no, auntie," Musa said politely. "She's not pregnant." He placed his hand on Fatou's shoulder and said, "This one. This is Fatou. She is pregnant. That is Jane." He then turned to Issa, who was standing behind him, and shoved him forward.

"Introduce." He told Issa with a smile.

"Your wife, eh?" Aunt Caroline asked with a look of pride.

Issa just looked around the room dumbfounded. We all looked back at him and waited for his response as he tried to maintain this sweet moment without revealing to his modest aunties that he was a sloppy cheat.

While Jelaney and Musa snickered, Baturu raised his eyebrows and prodded Issa with, "Yes?"

I waited patiently too, knowing that any response was bound to be hilarious.

"Don't be shy!" Aunt Caroline insisted. She then grabbed my arm and asked, "And who's beautiful wife is this?"

Once again, all eyes fell on Issa and relished his discomfort. Musa, barely able to contain his laughter, pointed toward me with both hands, encouraging Issa to speak up.

The aunties picked up on our cues and came to their own conclusion.

"Your *second* wife?" Aunt Edna asked. "The little one is the biggest man!" She teased.

Before any of us had a chance to correct her, they insisted that we get comfortable inside the house and get ready for a meal.

"We had a wonderful catch today!" Aunt Caroline continued. "More fish than we knew what to do with and even shrimp from a neighbor. I didn't know why we were given such things until just now. The Lord provided."

Aunt Edna added, "I was already making country chop and planning to invite some neighbors over. It's about time we go and get them. Everyone will be so happy to see that you've returned to us."

"Uh, we were hoping that we'd have more time to catch up… privately." Issa said.

The aunties looked confused.

"I'm afraid that we did not come here under the most ideal circumstances." Musa said. "It would be best if we don't draw any attention to ourselves."

Without reacting too quickly, the aunties sat up straight in their chairs and calmly waited for further explanation. It was as if they were already prepared with an understanding that a simple, sentimental reunion with their nephews was too good to be true. There had to be more. There must be some catch.

"Alright," their eyes said, *"why are you really here?"*

"The ghosts from that war are restless." Issa said. "And they are preventing us from resting. They have haunted us all the way to the U.S."

"We're not sure if you know about all that our fathers were involved in," Baturu said.

The aunties nodded. "We know enough."

"We need a safe haven," Issa said. "especially for Fatou, while we try to resolve things for good."

Aunt Edna let out a long sigh and then looked over at Aunt Caroline who was hanging onto their every word with a furrowed brow and one palm on her cheek.

"I won't question you." Aunt Edna responded. "You've come all this way… with a pregnant woman. I assume that this is what has to be done. Please be careful and use your very best judgement."

That was, seemingly, all that needed to be said about the purpose for our visit, until later that evening after dinner. We gathered around for coffee in the small courtyard that sat in the middle of the cluster of structures which made up the house. Aunt Caroline happily joined us with an armful of photo albums.

She carefully sat the albums down on a table by allowing them to slid down the arm that she was holding them with. It was then that I realized that she had only used her right hand throughout the entire afternoon. The left was always conveniently covered beneath a long piece of fabric that she kept draped over her shoulders.

As we all focused our attention on her, she slowly removed her arm from beneath the fabric and looked up at us with a reassuring smile. She rubbed her left shoulder, gently traced her fingers down her arm, which had been amputated from the elbow down, and placed her right hand in her lap.

"When they came here," She began, "I was certain that we were all going to die. I thought for sure that they knew— who we were, who our family was, about the money. I didn't realize that it was the children that they simply wanted to terrorize."

"Many of the children were Mandinka." Aunt Edna said. "There was absolutely nowhere to run. This was the safest place they had found."

Aunt Caroline lifted one of the photo albums and started thumbing through it. "We had built a fine place for them, just me and Edna, with our own hands. Some local guys helped us with supplies. We did the work, though... Those amputations were supposed to render us useless, to make the children useless."

"After we were attacked," Aunt Edna said, "there were a few nursing students and one doctor who insisted on staying with us to help treat the children. They never left, they are still here. The children grew up and made whatever attempts they could at finding a future in Monrovia or someplace... other than here."

"I am so happy that you all had the chance to escape then." Aunt Caroline said. "My greatest concern was that you all would have the chance to live full lives and not be stifled by such things."

"And yet you are back." Aunt Edna said abruptly. "Please, do not let your escape be in vain. Many of the fighters have receded back into society, including some of the worst offenders. Eventually everyone just wanted peace. But your enemies are exceptional."

"We understand." Musa assured them.

The photo albums were full of sights around the town of Harper.

"Years ago," Aunt Caroline pointed out, "this place was a jewel of Liberia. There was Tubman University, a cherished soccer stadium and museum, and churches. It was a place where residents and visitors expected to experience the best that the country had to offer— nice, spacious homes with indoor plumbing, electricity, nice roads, a respectable community of believers. The dark side of things was that the place was off limits to anyone but Americos. They didn't want natives living here. Anyhow, even now, the beaches are among the most lovely. The water temperature is warm year round."

"Jane is from America, Auntie." Musa added.

"Do you know our history, Jane?" Aunt Caroline asked me. She waved her finger between her and me as if "our history" was a shared one.

"I have to admit, I don't know much, except that the nation was formally founded by ex-slaves from America."

"Some of them very well may have been related to your ancestors. You might be returning home, too. "

***

After everyone finished their coffee, I chose to stay in the courtyard a little longer. There were several oil lamps burning around the house and a couple on the courtyard table. With no electricity, the distinct hum of appliances was absent. There was no noisy refrigerator compressor, no running dishwasher, no air conditioner pumping in the background. There was no car noise or chatter of people coming and going in the night.

Back in Philly, there were times when I longed for this kind of silence. And there were several times over the years when bad hurricanes hovered over my home town in Virginia forcing everyone into quiet contemplation and cooking with microwaves connected to car battery adapters. I never did mind it. The sudden dead silence and stillness were always such a relief.

I took notice of the sky as Issa came back out into the courtyard to check on me.

"Don't you ever miss this?" I asked him. "I really miss seeing stars. Back home, with all the light pollution, I can barely see any at all, even on the Eastern Shore. But here, they're countless. It's a crime to not be able to see stars like this."

He looked at me and then up at the sky.

"I wanna see the beach." I said.

"This isn't a holiday, Jane." Issa chuckled. "We don't have the luxury of squeezing in a beach excursion."

"I mean I want to see it now. Right now." I insisted. "It's right there. I can hear the waves. The last time I saw stars like this was in Tanzania, but it wasn't above the ocean... I want to see them over the ocean."

I could feel him staring at me, possibly in confusion or disbelief. After a moment of silence, he gave in.

"Okay, come on."

We passed by Jelaney and Musa who were talking on the front stoop as we headed out.

"W-where are you two going?" Musa asked.

"It's okay, Issa said. "We won't be gone long. She... she wants to see the beach."

Suspicion showed on Musa's face, but he relaxed somewhat when Issa insisted,

"She just wants to see the beach."

We walked around to the back of the house and cut through a field of sparse underbrush and palm trees. The ground was soft and sandy, and the smell of saltwater was in the air. There was only a crescent-shaped sliver of a moon hanging in the sky, but it was enough to provide some light for our short trek.

"It only takes a little light to break up the deepest darkness." I thought.

Within minutes we were facing the Atlantic Ocean. I sat down and folded my arms over my knees and stared ahead. Issa did the same. I wondered if being so disconnected from the night sky, the way I was back home, could have a tangible, negative impact on one's psyche. How could it not? Being able to see the universe with a simple glance upward is an irreplaceable part of the human experience.

"Look, there was a good reason why I held onto you." he started.

"Oh, Jesus! Will you just let me enjoy this." I said.

"It was a fair reason, in spite of my relationship with Fatou."

"I bet if you give me one good guess, I could figure out what that reason was." I said.

He shook his head. "No… After escaping what was happening here, what our future could have been, I started to believe that a much bigger, much better life was possible…You and Fatou are two very different women. When I met you, I could see that you were strong, determined. There's plenty of craziness about you, but I could see you working your way through it. After you told me what happened with you and Jack in Bermuda, I thought, '*This is a woman who can deal with some real shit. She's gonna be something one of these days.'* "

I let him keep going, because I was still admiring the sky and didn't want to be distracted from it by my own talking. I also wanted to know what Issa had been thinking.

"Fatou's different." He went on. "We could always count on each other. I always thought it was possible that I might have a future with her... Now that she's safe in there, I assure you she will be happy not to venture back out of those walls again until every single one of those rebel guys are taken care of. You two are different."

"So, why not have both?" I asked facetiously.

"I never meant to put you in harm's way, Jane... but you're here now, and we need your help."

"Yeah," I said, "I guess I need yours too, like before."

I was willing to admit my own vulnerability, but I still wanted to probe a little deeper on the subject of his relationships.

"Who are you kidding, anyway," I asked. "You really fancy yourself a family man?"

He looked shocked. "That's my ultimate goal. That's what you do. You go to school, stabilize yourself, you get married, have children, live respectably—"

"Only, you already kinda slipped up on that part. Got a few items on that list out of order, right?"

He laughed. "Look, I asked you early on if you could see a future with me and you said no."

"Get outta here!" I argued.

"This is exactly what you said. You said your Christian beliefs would not allow you to marry a Muslim."

"That's your excuse?" I asked. "C'mon man."

"What's yours?" he asked.

I refused to answer that question but responded, *"I'm* not pregnant. You know, even though I may have some difficulty adhering to my beliefs, I try not to pile up too many indiscretions."

"Now you must be kidding *me!"* he said.

"Seriously, we each experience a dark night of the soul at some point. That doesn't mean I'm not still committed."

"Hmm. Still committed. More like still afraid."

"What?"

"I get it." He answered. "Religion is a good thing. It's very much a means to an end. Devotion focuses the mind, helps a person develop discipline. Prayer has a similar effect to meditation, helping you regain or maintain psychological balance. The problem comes in when you take those books too literally."

"Here you go."

"It's intended to have a metaphorical meaning. You still have to think critically."

"It's not about intellect, Issa. It's about faith, faith in a God who is much bigger than your intellect."

"God gave you your intellect. God *is* your intellect."

"It is about faith and obedience to God, not about thin—"

"Not about thinking?" he asked abruptly. "This is your spirit, your life, your afterlife. Of all the times when one would need to think... this is it."

"I... I didn't mean that one shouldn't think... it... whatever."

Admittedly his statements caught me off guard. For the last decade, I had only read the Bible with others looking over my shoulder telling me what it all meant, reassuring me that this path was the correct one and that there was no need to consider another.

"Have you ever wondered if what you're truly exercising is faith?" he asked. "I've seen the way you force yourself to read that book, fighting off sleep. You look damn near pissed off when you have to get up on Sunday mornings."

"What are you trying to say?" I asked.

He lowered his head and his voice respectfully, almost as if trying to take the edge off his words.

"I don't think it's faith. I think it's fear. Your devotion doesn't make you happy. It just keeps you in check—barely. It doesn't even line up with who you are, your personality. It's not you. Being restricted, toeing the line, doing what you're told. That's not you, not the real you. I'm not trying to make you change your religion or anything. But I've seen what you can do when you're not afraid and how stagnant you become when you are."

"It's interesting that we're talking about this," I said. "because I have been thinking about some things that have to do with my upbringing and what I was taught, about faith and the Bible."

"Yeah?"

"Yeah… well, I've always been taught, and I've always really believed that Jesus is the one we can rely on, the one who makes everything whole."

"Um hmm."

"We're taught that we can lay everything at his feet, including all our faults and missteps."

"Right."

"But resting on that alone doesn't create *any* necessary change or forward progress in a person's life…. It's only a comfort … a pacifier for the person casting off their pain. We still have to do the *work* of correcting our wrongs, developing our character, improving our circumstances."

Issa leaned back and looked out over the water as I continued. My heart beat a little faster as I made room for a flow of thoughts that I had stifled too many times before.

"My belief system...appears to be one... that rewards fear. It trains you into a victim state of mind and then presents itself as the rescuer. *'You're alone and afraid, right'*, it asks. *'You're broken, you're sinful, you're completely unworthy'*, it tells you. *'But here is the fix'*, it says. Here is your refuge. Here's a God who will allay all your fears and fight your battles.

"Then once you commit to the faith, you're told that the world hates you, that it hates all that you stand for. It's you and the Lord against world— the sinful, useless world where nothing good exists and all is of the devil. Once again, you are a victim, but of *persecution* this time. And, again, the only fix is this faith. Faith or certain destruction are the only options— which really means you don't have any choice. There's always the fear of destruction... cloaked as faith.

"I was a happy kid, a free kid. But somewhere along the way I became very afraid. Afraid of messing up. There seemed to be so many traps. I grew up during the crack epidemic. While you and your family were fleeing real persecution and civil war here, the war on drugs was being waged in my world. Not quite the same kind of mayhem, I know, but it was a very serious situation, and much more covert.

"We heard our fair share of gunfire. I had cousins in and out of jail, always fighting or getting into some kind of trouble. One of my older cousins got into this fight one time when I was a kid. We all got out of the car after coming from the store. Out of nowhere, this girl from around the way came running up on my cousin, fussing about some boyfriend of hers that my cousin was messing with. They started fighting and that girl latched onto my cousin's bottom lip with her *teeth*. Tried to rip her lip right off. Wild! This was in my Grandma Sadie's neighborhood where any car that pulled up would be greeted by the welcoming committee of street pharmacists who immediately asked you your drug of choice."

Issa nodded, totally unsurprised, and continued listening.

"My mom is one of ten, and half of them were strung out back then. Three of the boys and two of the girls. You already know about my dad. We watched our aunts and uncles turn into walking skeletons, overheard them scheming to rob somebody or to make fiend loans for extra cash. I saw my aunt walk the streets, knowing where she was headed and why. One time two or three of them showed up on our doorstep, glassy-eyed, ready for a fight with my dad, demanding back a TV and radio that they just gave us a few months before, so they could be pawned for drug money. In high school, on the way to school mornings, I waited for the bus right next to my dad's car for months. It wasn't drivable because the back window had been blown out by a drug dealer whose bullet my dad had narrowly escaped.

"It seems crazy, but none of that scared me, at least not much. I wasn't afraid of getting shot or strung out or harmed by anything related to that kind of life. All that was just noise. I was so detached from it because I had a one track mind, and I had already chosen not to go that route. I had been taught that God was bigger than all of that, and so *He* was the one that I feared. I became afraid of making God angry, of not living up to my own potential. It seemed like so many people around me had not lived up to anywhere near their potential. It was such a shame, a colossal waste."

"Hmm." Issa said. "Well… spending your whole life trying to avoid pissing God off is like hiding in a closet from Michael Myers and holding back a fart."

I burst out laughing. "What?!"

"You know it's true." he said. "Especially since God is supposedly so easily angered. You're bound to let one slip. Why did you wanna come out here so badly?"

"The ocean is so big," I explained. "It seems never-ending, limitless. And the darkness…I like the uncertainty of it, the mystery of it. Oddly, that makes me feel safe, like I'm right at home. Whenever I'd escape classes for the semester and drive down Route 13 to visit my family, my favorite part of the trip was driving through the Eastern Shore after dark. Watching the trees become a collective black mass, then floating out over the shiny, inky Chesapeake bay. It was spooky…and thrilling. Even better in the rain."

Issa shook his head, but grinned the way he usually did when conceding to my eccentricity.

"The darkness has the power to take away inhibitions and fears, if you let it, if you face it. It's embracing the unknown. Like the darkness that exists beyond that sky, it represents infinite potential. It's like falling asleep, too, you know… No wonder we sleep at night. To think that you can access the keys to the universe by just embracing the darkness or falling asleep."

"We promised our parents we would come back," he said. "but there was too much of 'the unknown'. That war, the horrors that humans create right here on earth, that's hell."

"Yeah." I agreed. "The horrors we create are apparently worse than any ideas of the afterlife that we could ever contrive to keep ourselves in check... Dante's inferno my ass."

I tried tossing a rock far ahead into the ocean while Issa looked at me. He was probably just as surprised by my revelation as I was. I felt like scales were falling from my eyes, and he was watching it happen.

He went on. "We promised each other that we wouldn't touch that money until we could come back here and use it to help rebuild the country. Hey, when we're older, if I invite you back here, will you come see me and hang out?"

"Depends on what you mean by 'hang out'."

"You know what I mean. Maybe just come see the sights, meet some of my people, enjoy yourself and this place, under better circumstances."

"Hmmm, what if I'm married by then? Can I bring my husband and kids with me?"

His face returned to that typically dry and dismissive expression, then he looked back at the ocean.

"Your husband... Come on, we should probably head back."

14

The next morning, we all met in the courtyard for breakfast and talked about what needed to happen next. Now that we had made it safely to Liberia and Fatou could settle into a secure location, we had to focus on Monrovia. Musa laid out the basics.

"We need to get to Monrovia as quickly as possible, but we need to do it without being detected. If we drive, any number of people are bound to see us and start talking, even if they're not sure who we are. If those guys are back here and they really have their ears to the ground— which I'm sure they will— they'll be on our trail in no time."

"How will you have any way of knowing whether or not they're back here?" Fatou asked.

"Even if they're not, they have guys who are always here, and we don't know how many people they're working with."

"Tell me *more* good news." I said in frustration.

"Listen," Musa went on, "I sent Jelaney to an internet café a little ways from here so that he could contact our friend in Philly. Eleanor will be able to tell him what direction they've gone in. My guess is they've already left Philly since we're all gone. The question is, did they make some other stop along the way, or come straight here for us."

"It's highly likely that they'd be headed for Monrovia." Baturu added. "Deana will be there soon, and they know we'll probably be there eventually."

"The roads are too risky, especially with all the rain." Musa continued. "What if we break down? We don't have weapons, and a bunch of unfamiliar guys buying some around here would look suspicious. We don't know anyone here. Again, people would talk. We can't get weapons until we can make a discrete connection with someone we know in Monrovia. And the only other option for getting there is by boat."

Issa looked distressed.

"How long will that take?" Fatou asked.

Musa let out a long sigh. "With a small boat... three to six days."

Baturu nodded while Issa threw his head back in anguish.

"A cruise along the Liberian coastline in a dinghy. Why not?" I said.

"Don't start with the jokes, Jane." Issa said. "I do not consider this a viable option."

"Issa, we have no other choice." Baturu said.

"I am not going on a boat for six days."

"Issa, it could be much less, depending."

"I'm not getting on a boat."

"We have no other choice!"

"I won't do it."

"Issa, you will!" Baturu insisted.

"No I won't."

"Dammit, you will!!"

They spent the next several seconds pushing and shoving each other, yelling, "I won't!" and "You damn well will!" until Musa stepped in and shut them up.

"Issa," he said. "You are going. We are all getting on that boat."

"*What* boat?" I asked.

Musa and Baturu hesitated then looked at me. "We're not sure yet." Musa replied.

"Three to six days is the amount of time it takes some canoes to get there."

"CANOES!" Fatou cried.

"Let me finish." Musa pleaded. "Some small boat is a last resort, but not canoes. Of course we're not taking canoes."

"Jesus, then why even bring up canoes?" Issa asked.

"He was just making a point." Baturu shouted. "That's how long it takes small boats to get from here to Monrovia."

"Okay, let's focus." Musa said.

We all waited for him to continue.

"So?" Issa prodded.

"The MV Caterina." Baturu said. "It's involved with the UN peacekeeping mission. It sails between here and Monrovia every two weeks."

"Two weeks!" Issa said.

"It's due for a stop here in one week." Musa said. "And we cannot miss it. By way of the Caterina, we can get to Monrovia in less than a day."

"And we do what in the meantime?" I asked.

"Lay low." he responded. "Keep yourself occupied inside the compound. Try not to venture out unless we absolutely have to."

"An entire week 'til Monrovia?" Issa asked nervously. "Anything can happen in that time."

"Not if you're smart." Baturu snapped.

"You call trying to hitch a ride on a military patrol vessel full of soldiers and cops who intend to prevent illegal immigration *smart*?" Issa asked.

"Issa, I am tired of your whining! Every journey can't be a posh ride in a luxury locomotive!"

"You, the transport man!" Issa shouted back, "So far you've managed to downgrade us to common car thieves. Now trafficking! You can't find one discreet and legal means of travel, one decent vehicle?"

"The *roads,* Issa." Musa reminded him.

"Sitting around here for an entire week, waiting to be hunted down?" Issa put his hand in his pockets and shook his head in defiance to the idea.

"Well more time, at this point, could help us out, right?" I asked. "I mean, if we show up exactly when they're expecting us, won't they be on high alert anyway?"

"She has a point, Issa." Baturu said. "Definitely."

"If we're able to make it onto the UN ship— and please do explain to me how the hell you plan to pull that off— that's extra cover for us. We'll have safe travel there and, possibly, a safer means of transitioning off the boat and into wherever our destination is in Monrovia."

"What do you mean?" Issa asked me.

"With a day to kill on that boat, maybe we can finagle an escort to the AfDB headquarters out of one of the soldiers. We get there and let Deana know the danger we're in, then we'll have the backing of government agencies to keep us safe. She can even pull some strings to get those guys off our trail."

"If only it could be so easy to get that help." Issa said. "Do you have any idea how many people we'd have to pay off along the way just to keep them from handing us over to the cops?"

"It's actually not too far-fetched." Musa argued. "Now, I'm not interested in alerting the authorities. They just can't be trusted. But I do think that Deana can help provide cover while we find out where these guys are. And she can help us get some supplies along the way."

"We'll have to dig into your accounts and find out where the guys are who have been tampering with them, see how recently they've accessed them." I said. "But we'll have to do it fast, if those guys are still monitoring them."

"About that money," Fatou jumped in, "why even go through all of this. If they can tamper with all these accounts, then they can access the money. Why not just take it and leave us alone?"

"They want us dead, Fatou." Issa said. "It's not only about the money."

"Plus most of the money is in offshore accounts." Musa continued. "They're more secure, harder to access... but I am surprised they haven't at least tried. Something's preventing them from making an attempt."

"What do you think that is?" Baturu asked.

"I don't know."

Musa and Issa sat back in chairs across from each other and folded their arms. They looked at each other as if the same idea was beginning to form in their minds.

"Jajah." They said simultaneously.

"Maybe he's holding them off." Musa said.

Issa sat up as if energized by the idea and said, "We have to contact him right away. Is Jelaney getting some phones out there too?"

"Yeah," Musa said. "But they'll be useless while we're out here with no signal."

"We may have to venture out again and contact him." Issa said. "Better for him to know ahead of our arrival."

All three of the guys nodded in confidence.

"Okay," I said, "so what do we do after we make contact? After we speak with Deana and get all this information from Jajah and all that? Am I missing something here, because it sounds like we won't have much help from the authorities, and Deana and Jajah are only helping us with paperwork... You mentioned weapons."

Musa shifted in his chair and gave me a slightly nervous glance.

"What you guys are getting ready for is some kind of showdown, isn't it?"

Musa and Baturu looked away.

"Just say it. You want to make sure the accounts are secure, and then you want to hunt these guys down and kill them!"

"Well... not *guys*." Baturu finally said. "One guy... or just two guys in particular."

"Three tops." Issa agreed.

"Maybe four, but that's it." Musa tried to assure me.

"Anybody wanna go for five?" I shook my head in disbelief. "Do you even have a clue who all these guys are?"

"We know who they are." Issa said.

"They're the friends of that rebel guy who Jelaney's father tried to kill." Musa said. "A few years ago, we heard that two of them had fallen ill and that one was in prison. Hopefully, at least the two sick ones died off."

I looked into each one of their faces and was hard-pressed to picture a murderer.

"Are you all ready for this? I mean, really? You are talking about the premeditated hunting down and killing of people. Do you have any idea how hard that is to do, even if it's an *accident*? And these are supposedly vicious, cold-blooded cannibals. You guys fled the war, you're college boys, businessmen. You're not killers!"

"Jane," Issa replied, "we don't have any other choice. We promised to come back here years ago to help rebuild our country. And, honestly, we tried to avoid it. But we have to face this now. If we do, then that will make it possible for us to keep our promise later, when we're ready."

Their minds were made up. That was clear. The prospect of a bloody confrontation crystalized in my imagination and horrified me. I couldn't help but resent the fact that Issa had allowed me to haphazardly come upon all this, had allowed me to pursue a job at the same bank where he worked with an attorney who worked for his family. He had insisted that I live with him, which led to me being irreversibly tangled up in this mess.

"You sneaky son of a bitch." I said looking coldly into his eyes.

He looked baffled.

"You lying, conniving, black-hearted piece of—"

"What the hell is wrong with you?" he asked angrily.

"What am I? A pawn? Some kind of buffer between you and these guys, this crisis? You thought you'd get me tangled up in this and bring me here so I could help with the cause, be your guard dog. Bunch of cowards, you guys aren't killers. If you were, you would have picked off every one of those thugs back in Philly when you had the chance. *I'm* the only killer here!"

"This chick is losing it." Baturu mumbled.

Issa stood up and moved toward me. "Calm down, Jane."

"Jane, please." Fatou said. "It's not at all what you think. He had no intention of harming you."

"Don't tell me what to do! Don't any of you cowards tell me what to do!"

"Jane, you have this all wrong. Just sit down." Issa insisted.

"No!"

"We have a plan." Musa said. "We can fix this. Issa never intended for you to be involved. Just think rationally."

As Issa went to grab my arm, I picked up a slender, wooden statue that was sitting next to my chair and swung it into the air.

"Don't touch me!"

Issa tried to grab my waist, and I stomped on his foot while Musa dodged the swinging statue in an effort to take it from me. The statue cracked Musa over the back, and I made a run for it as he fell to the ground.

"Get up and help us!" Musa shouted while Baturu sat shaking his head.

On the way out the front door, I passed Jelaney who was returning from the internet café in a ball cap and sun shades disguise. He was totally confused by my shooting past him and into the yard.

"Go get her, you idiot!" Issa said to him as he limped up behind us.

While they were still figuring out how to get themselves together, I broke through the palm trees that Issa and I had passed through the night before on the way to the beach. When I hit the shore, I ran alongside it until the heat of the sun and sand forced me to slow down.

Ahead, there was another cluster of trees and shrubs that I could take refuge in until I figured out some miracle to get me out of this situation. I headed in their direction and rested among them.

Eventually, I could see Baturu and Issa bringing up the rear, panting, squinting, and holding their sides. They followed my tracks to the trees where I was hiding and waited just outside them.

"Are you gonna come out?" Baturu asked. His exhaustion seemed more mental than physical.

"No."

"You will eventually." he sighed. He flopped down on the sand and waited.

"You will NOW." Issa said, then he walked into the trees over to where I was sitting. "Jane, come on."

I ignored him.

"Jane!" he pleaded with hands outstretched.

I didn't say a word.

"You know there are snakes in here." he said

"I'm sitting right in front of one!" I yelled, then I settled back onto the sand.

He paced back and forth, pausing every once in a while to stare at me. He finally gave up and sat down.

"I already told you," he started, "I did not purposefully involve you in this situation. I had no intention of ever putting you in harm's way."

I shook my head in refusal.

"You can think whatever else you want to think of me, Jane, but that just isn't true. I didn't tell you everything, because we were still trying to figure things out ourselves. What would be the point in scaring you to death if we didn't have any solutions?"

I said nothing.

"Deana did this to you."

I looked into his eyes and tried to determine if they looked sincere.

"I didn't know how to fix it. I didn't tell you at first, because I thought that would have been one more thing to cause you stress."

"What do you mean, Deana did this? How?"

"When I put in a word for you at the bank, she made sure you got the job. I thought it was great. If it worked out you could gain experience with commercial real estate funding and build on your expertise in that area. I didn't think that you would be doing any pertinent work for her, because you said she handled most of her own files. But it looks like she was using your computer's IP address whenever she sent messages or did any work related to our business and our accounts. Any transaction that she processed, every account number or password that she used, was transmitted via the IP address from your work computer."

"Why would she do that?" I said.

"Deana's a crook, and she thinks she has us fooled. She's planning to steal from us and she's trying very hard to cover her tracks. She didn't care if those guys saw a trail from your IP address and came after you. She wanted it that way. She's only planning to be in Monrovia for two weeks. After that, she's settling into the AfDB headquarters in Tunisia."

He stood back up and extended his hand toward me before helping me off the ground.

"Or at least she thinks she is."

I couldn't believe what I was hearing. My relationship with Deana had not been particularly close, but to think she'd sell me up the river like this, using me as a cover so she could make off with the guys' money, was utterly foul.

"Let's catch that boat." I said.

We all left the beach and silently made our way back to the house.

15

I don't think any of us had any idea how interesting one week pinned up in the aunties' house could get. Not only were we in hiding from the rebels, but we were also kept indoors most days by the powerful, rainy season storms.

Understandably, the aunties were overjoyed to have a house full of young people again, especially their long lost nephews, but they immediately started calling us "Pekin", and treating us like the kids they had cared for in the orphanage. It was like they were pretending the orphanage was open all over again, especially Aunt Caroline. (It seemed more like Aunt Edna followed her lead and was simply going along with everything to indulge her sentimentality.)

They doted on each of us, right down to instinctively wiping the mouth of whichever one of us happened to be sitting next to them during a meal. They didn't miss an opportunity to pull out those photo albums and tell us the same stories of what Harper used to be. And each night, just after sunset, they insisted that we "calm down", say our prayers and prepare to sleep. Issa would do as they asked, since it was Ramadan, and he was making an attempt at spiritual contemplation after breaking fast. The rest of us quieted down out of respect, but as soon as they were asleep, we resumed our activities into the night.

They fed us like little pigs that they were trying to fatten up, and every day was like a holiday when it came to food. To avoid drawing attention to themselves in the markets, they went fishing for meat instead and brought back large amounts of fish for lunch and dinner. On a couple of days, they even brought back lobster.

Each of us was given a chore, which was actually a relief in that it gave us something to do and kept the guys from annoying each other and bickering. We all cleaned and fought back the mud that threatened to overtake the floors. Issa and Jelaney gathered firewood along with small sticks that Fatou and I used to make mulch for the pineapple plants. These would protect them from soil erosion. We also helped with the laundry and cooking. Musa and Baturu built and managed the small fire pit in the back used for burning trash at the end of each day.

In our free time, Fatou and I pored over old books which were piled up in shelves that the aunties had built into the walls. Each bedroom had them, so during the day, we'd go from room to room perusing the collections and picking a favorite. Aunt Caroline was adamant about making sure that we returned each book before the end of a day, so we made sure to put each one back before everyone went to sleep.

On our third night, I happened to be returning a book to Jelaney and Musa's room while they finished up dinner.

I got carried away flipping through a new one when Musa walked through the curtained entry and found me there.

"What's that one about?" he asked, startling me so badly I almost dropped the book.

"Um, uh, it's an oceanography book. Has a lot of cool pictures. All the good science books are in you guys' rooms. We have art books, mostly. Art and literature."

"I thought art and literature would be right down your alley. That's why we took this room." he said.

"They are, but I'm into science, too. Thanks, by the way. There's a lot of good reading material around here, thank goodness."

"Lots of interests. You're curious." Musa noted. "Eh, I guess that can be entertaining, but I'm not a huge reader."

"Then I hope you're not bored out of your mind." I said.

"Not at all." He said. "My mind is plenty busy."

"I guess it would be under these circumstances."

"Actually, I'm thinking about some other things. I'm just organizing a few ideas in my mind for moving forward with my career once we get back to Philly."

"Yeah, I never did find out. What do you do?"

"Baturu and I are working on setting up a fund to provide financial resources for small businesses."

"Ah, venture capitalists. Will you also be advising startups?"

"Possibly, down the line. We've been trying to get Issa on board too, but seems he likes to play it safe. My risk tolerance is a bit higher than his, as you can probably tell."

He took a couple of steps closer to me and said, "I'm not the type to hedge my bets quite so heavily."

"Don't you think someone in your line of work should hedge his bets pretty well?"

"Not when I know what I'm doing... and I usually do."

"Okay, Geez, well, all of this must really be putting a damper on your plans."

"Not really. This is going to work out. And when it does, we'll go back and move on."

I nodded in agreement, admiring his optimism. Then I assumed that he was about to get into bed, because he started to take off his shirt. I rose to leave, but he kept talking, catching me a little off guard.

"With so many of us here, you hardly need those books to keep you entertained. Did you hear Baturu out in the kitchen? He DJs on the side, and now he and Jelaney think they're rappers, too."

I used my laughter as an excuse to avert my eyes from his flawless chest as he stood in front of me half naked and preparing to take off his pants.

"I did, I did. They're actually not bad. Better than a handful of those fools getting paid really good money for half as much talent."

He paused with his hands on his hips and a cool smile on his face.

"Well, I guess I'll let you get some rest." I said.

"What's the hurry? It's not late. I wasn't planning on sleeping yet or anything, just changing clothes."

"Yeah, but maybe Jelaney will be going to bed soon or something. I probably shouldn't be all up in your room if he does. Plus I'm kinda hungry. Gonna grab a snack."

My attempt at modesty and a quick exit didn't seem to faze him.

"You don't strike me as a shy type." he said.

"You didn't strike me as the type who would try to go after his brother's girl. And really? You think you just gon' strip right here, right now and that'll be it? You're as bad as Issa. He just whips it out and leaves it at that."

(I was curiously wondering if he'd do the same.)

He corrected me. "Ex girl."

"That's not the point."

"Issa's still doing that crap?" he asked. "Geez, you poor woman!"

Without even fully noticing the awkward situation that he was entering, Jelaney scooted into the room quickly, grabbed his shoes, and headed back toward the entry.

"Rained stopped. We'll be out back. Issa found a football." he said.

I looked back up at Musa and knew that there was no way that I was going to allow myself to get reeled in by him... at least not so quickly. Even if Issa and I were no longer together and Musa was the strong, tall, leader of the bunch with the gorgeous smile, I couldn't hop from one brother to another, especially not in the midst of all this other insanity- could I?

"Goodnight, Musa." I said before politely leaving.

When I was just outside the room, he responded, "Almost."

***

Out in the backyard, Issa had already succumbed to his aversion to strenuous activity and was sitting out the game.

"That was quick." I said. "Feet bothering you?"

He took off one shoe and rubbed his foot then gave me a pitiful look.

"Don't even think about it." I said. "Your wife's around here somewhere."

"Yeah, she's playing." He pointed out into the yard where Fatou was just barely getting the best of Jelaney.

"Come on, Jane!" She yelled to me. "I need a teammate."

"Is this a good idea for you?" I asked her.

"Exercise? Sure. But the ball stays on the ground." She said. "No lobs, no head shots, you know."

I stood in front of Baturu to block him and got ready for a pass from Fatou.

"Oh, I get the crazy one on defense?" he asked.

I rolled my eyes at him before taking the ball down the yard. Jelaney intercepted it right before I could make the goal.

"Almost." Musa said with a cheeky grin. He was still shirtless, but now sitting next to Issa with his arms folded, enjoying the entertainment.

"You know where we should go after this?" Jelaney asked while preparing to kick the ball back in. "Cabo Verde!"

"Yeah, man!" Baturu agreed. "When all this shit is over with, we should just spend a week there, chilling out. Hang out on the beaches and meet some girls."

"What's Cabo Verde?" I asked Fatou.

"It's a group of islands just off the coast of West Africa, close to Senegal. Some people call it little Brazil. It was colonized by the Portuguese."

"I have had enough of traveling." Issa said. "I personally would have no problem with going back to Philly, back to work, and right back to that sorry apartment. I'd do it gladly!"

"You think we can just go back to the bank after confronting Deana?" I asked. "Sliding back into business as usual is not going to be easy after all this."

"Listen to your wife, Issa." Musa said. "She knows what it's like to escape disaster like that and jump right back into everyday life. That's a hard thing to do."

I stopped and stared at him, wondering what he meant. I figured that Issa told him something about my run-in with Jack several years earlier, but I didn't think that was really any of his business.

He went on, "Why not show the ladies a good time for all their trouble. You know Jane loves the beach."

I ignored his attempt to put me on the spot and kept my eye on the ball. So he tried harder for some attention. I focused on the game to make him think I wasn't listening, but I could still hear some of what they were saying.

"Man, Issa, I didn't know how you were gonna explain to aunties that you and Fatou aren't sharing a room. Her and Jane in the same room while you bunk with Baturu? But I guess if you just keep it out of their sight, you won't have to explain yourself. Gonna have to be clever."

Issa laughed off his comment.

"More clever than you've been so far, little brother." Musa added.

"Oh yeah?" Issa asked. The grin on his face showed that he was amused by Musa's taunting. "Well, how would you suggest I handle the situation?"

"Eh, you know aunties are already so concerned for our well-being. Put their minds at ease and behave like a contented family. Make peace. Be with your wife. Jane can just bunk with someone else. Of course, you would have to divulge that *she's* not your wife."

"Oh really," Issa said. "And who might you suggest she bunk with instead? I'd hate for her to have to deal with being... uncomfortable here, on top of everything else."

"Ah! I'm a perfect gentleman. She'd have the utmost comfort." Musa said.

"Really man, don't you have anything better to do?" Issa asked.

"Don't *you*?" Musa responded.

Fatou stopped for a sip of water and said, "He can try and bunk with me if he wants. You'd all have to explain his sudden death."

Musa took over for Baturu and appointed himself as my opponent. I was not impressed. Well, I pretended like I wasn't.

"Don't worry, I can handle the crazy ones." He told Baturu.

"Oh, you wanna see crazy?" I asked

He just nodded and prepared to block me.

As the ball came our way, I assured him, "Touch me and you will."

It was going to be a long four more days.

***

First thing in the morning, I awakened to a knock on the wall just outside our room.

"Yes, aunties?" I yelled while pulling on a long piece of material that they had given me to sleep and lounge in. I thought it may be them asking us to help with something around the house, but there was no answer. Whoever it was knocked again.

I stood by the door and asked, "Yes? Is that aunties?"

"It's Musa." he said with a touch of morning brightness.

"Yeeees?" I asked again.

"Good morning." He sang.

"Are you kidding me?"

"Aunties made breakfast already. I just thought I'd invite you and Fatou before these brutes destroy the meal. You know, in some instances, men do eat first."

"Yeah, okay. Well, we just woke up. We'll be out in a bit."

"Take your time." he said before walking away. "But not too much."

"Those guys are fucking savages." Fatou said while sitting up in bed.

"Tell me about it." I agreed.

"Do you like him at all?" She asked me.

I admitted, "A little bit. But I barely know him and his whole approach seems pretty sleazy. I'm not interested in being a hot topic among the brothers."

"Too late for that." She said. "But if you don't like him, just keep holding him off. Let him put that energy into the journey ahead."

"What are you gonna do about Issa?" I asked her. "Am I gonna be getting a really awkward invitation in a few months or just suddenly seeing your wedding pics on Facebook?"

"Ah!" she laughed. "You know, seriously, I never really saw myself marrying Issa. His attitude about love has just always been so nonchalant, so dry, so placid. I think life made him that way— nothing moves him. Loyalty is the one thing we share besides this baby. In some cases that's enough."

"But in your case it isn't?"

"Not for life… come on, you know what he's like in bed!" she said.

I could only nod in enthusiastic agreement.

"He's pragmatic and responsible in matters like these. I think we'll be good co-parents. I doubt it will hurt his feelings much."

"Have you told him yet?"

"…No."

"The man's not as cold-blooded as he seems, and he thinks you're a homebody." I said.

"Hmm." she said.

I gathered a few items and stepped through the curtain into the hallway on the way to the washroom, but before I could walk two steps, Issa popped his head out of his room and motioned for me to go back in mine.

"Wait! Wait!" he whispered.

"What?"

"The aunties!" he said.

I turned and saw Musa standing at the end of the hallway, curiously staring at us both. He kept his eyes on us and loudly greeted the aunties as they came around the corner.

"Oh, good morning, aunties!"

"Good morning, pee-key." Aunt Edna said.

"I hope you slept well." Aunt Caroline said to me. "We gave you all a little extra time this morning."

"Thank you Aunt Caroline. I rested very well. Do you need any help with anything before breakfast?"

"Oh, no, no, Jane. Just get dressed and enjoy. We've cut a few pineapples from the yard along with bananas, mangoes, and oranges for a nice fruit salad. We also made more gaaree and calla. You liked the garee yesterday, right?"

"Yes, it's a lot like cream of wheat back home. And the calla are like little doughnuts. I like them a lot."

"Yes, so you will enjoy! I hope you are not getting too lonely in this room by yourself."

I hesitated for a moment, "Uh—"

"Oh, how are you, Fatou?" Aunt Caroline asked as Fatou emerged from the room behind me. "W-why are you not with your husband? You girls must be getting along very well, having a morning girl talk."

Issa and I nodded nervously while Fatou remained expressionless.

"I was just telling Jane that a nice breakfast is waiting as soon as you are dressed." Aunt Caroline beamed with pride. "I even picked out a few baby names that we can all have fun going through while you eat. That is, in case you haven't already chosen to give him your husband's fine name. It's the Arabic equivalent of Jesus."

The aunties turned to walk away and Issa breathed a sigh of relief. Then Fatou blurted out,

"He's NOT my husband." Then she stormed back into the bedroom.

All of a sudden the aunties were looking back at Issa and me, expecting an explanation. Musa, now joined by Baturu, continued to stand by in amusement.

"Wha- what?" Aunt Edna said in confusion.

I had no idea what to say, and Issa just stood there with his mouth open.

"Explain, I beg!" she went on. "Issa, you and Fatou are not married?"

"No!" Fatou yelled from inside the room.

"Issa, are you the father of her child?"

"Yes." he admitted sheepishly.

"But you are not married?"

"No."

"Okay then," she said, "who is Jane? Is she also not your wife?"

"…No."

"Then who is she… speak up!"

"Fatou, Jane… Fatou and Jane are, were, my girlfriends."

"Which one is your girlfriend *now*?"

"Eh… neither, neither of them."

"Which one was your girlfriend before Fatou got belly?" Aunt Edna pressed.

"… Both of them."

"A lying two-timer!" Aunt Edna smacked Issa in the back of the head.

All of this must have been pretty entertaining for Musa, Baturu and Jelaney, who were watching from the end of the hall and tossing calla to each other for snacks.

"How did you get yourselves into this mess?" Aunt Caroline asked me.

"It's a long story, which I myself barely knew until very recently." I said.

"Well, let's see if we can't sort it out over breakfast." She said before she and Aunt Edna walked away.

At breakfast, as we all sat silently piling up our plates, Aunt Edna finally decided to break the ice.

"I knew he couldn't have acquired a second woman." she said. "He can barely hold a conversation with the first one."

Everyone began to laugh, except Issa.

"They aren't children anymore, Caroline. You may as well get used to that." she said.

Aunt Caroline looked a little sad and poked at her food.

"Well, you just better take care of your business." She said pointing at Issa. "Get them out of this mess and take care of business."

She went on to share some of the names that she was considering for Issa and Fatou's baby. Fatou seemed to be in a better mood and was pleased with some of the names. Issa joined in the discussion with a slight look of excitement on his face, although he did seem taken aback by Fatou's unwillingness to make eye contact with him. I, personally, was still a little sleepy.

From the corner of my eye, I could see Musa and Jelaney whispering to each other, but I chose to ignore them. Then Musa slid his otherwise untouched cup of coffee across the table to me.

"I don't like coffee very much. You can have mine."

Was this his way of trying to be sweet or funny? I couldn't help but giggle. It seemed childish in a cute way. We both tried to stop grinning when everyone looked to our end of the table to see where the giggling was coming from.

Once everyone had finished their second or third helping of food, the Aunties had us follow them through the main section of the house, up some steps, and into a little room just above the family space. They walked over to a closet with a trunk sitting on the floor and told us to gather around.

I was hoping they would present some interesting family heirlooms to the boys, and I was excited to see them. Well, I guess what they were about to present could be considered a bequest, but it definitely wasn't the typical type.

Aunt Edna hesitated for a moment then said, "When you got here, on the run for your lives, we didn't want to show you these at first. We only wanted you to feel safe, to feel like you had made it to a peaceful place where you are loved and taken care of, and where you don't have to worry about any fighting. These would only be a last resort."

Aunt Caroline added, "So much fighting has already taken place. You children should not have to endure anymore."

Aunt Edna went on, "But we understand that you have to defend yourselves. When you have no choice but to fight, you must have the proper weapons."

She lifted a decorative scarf which covered the trunk then opened it. Inside was a small arsenal. Admittedly, I was stunned (and sort of relieved) to see a number of handguns and two assault rifles along with plenty of ammunition. Then I got mental pictures of scenes from those documentaries that I'd watched over the years about war in some African country or another. Were these legacy firearms legitimately obtained or were the Aunties closet gangstas? I wondered how they purchased these weapons, who had fired them before, and who they had been fired upon.

"After what happened at the orphanage, we knew that we did not want to be helpless if such a thing should happen again." Aunt Caroline said. "We built this place ourselves, and we will defend it ourselves if we have to, no matter what the outcome!"

Bless her heart. Aunt Caroline meant that with every fiber of her being, and she sported a tightly balled up fist and the meanest grimace I've ever seen on a ninety-year-old woman to prove it. Her facial contortions rippled through her velvety wrinkles and made her look like a cross between Bruce Lee mid-kick and the Crypt Keeper.

Like the tragedy that they had endured, the expression did not suit her sweet and doting demeanor at all, and I hoped to God that she would never have to back up all that talk.

"We don't know if it will be feasible to take them with you. But— heaven forbid it— if you should need them while you're here, they are yours."

Aunt Edna brushed her palms across one another several times while they both repeated the phrase, "Heaven forbid it. Heaven forbid it."

When they left the room, we all looked at each other.

"Well," I asked, "Has anyone here ever used anything like this?"

"I think we all know how to shoot, generally. We learned when we were young." Baturu said. He gave Fatou a curious glance, and she quickly looked away. Understandably, the notion of a showdown at the aunties' house seemed to be making her very uncomfortable.

"We don't exactly have the ability to just go out back and practice." Musa said. He knelt down and hovered his hands over the weapons before reaching in and handing one to Issa. "We can at least familiarize ourselves with the feel of them, know how to transition from the safety mechanism, practice aiming. Then leave them right here in the meantime."

Quicker than anyone could stop him, Jelaney pointed one of the handguns toward a window and we all heard an empty click as he pulled it's trigger.

"What the hell is wrong with you, Jelaney?" Baturu yelled. He yanked the unloaded gun from Jelaney's hands and left him standing stunned with his hands frozen open.

"I-I didn't mean to touch the trigger. I was just looking through the sight." Jelaney said.

"Well, wait until you're not standing in a room full of people." Baturu said.

"You don't think we should travel with any?" Issa asked. "I mean, I know it will be risky to carry them on the boat to Monrovia, but how likely is it that we'll have access to weapons soon after we get there— weapons we won't have to hunt down and pay for?"

"Well," Musa responded, "whether or not we can pull that off depends on how well we can work the ship's crew. If yet another of Baturu's contacts turns out to be reliable, we may have significant help with our trip on the MV Caterina. Jelaney called him from the café."

Mention of another one of Baturu's "could be good, could be bad" connections left me irritated. That, plus the thought of these regular dudes toting guns around like some band of wannabe thugs, was too much for me. I still didn't have complete faith in their ability to withstand a fight with the rebels, and I was praying for a miracle. I walked out of the armory and escaped to my bedroom to read about sea creatures.

At sunset Musa showed up outside my room again.

"Hey... you gonna come back outta there?" he asked.

"Rather not."

"Hmm. Was it Issa and Fatou's reunion at breakfast, the guns, or me?"

"Ha! I am happy for Issa and Fatou having some peace. The guns themselves are the one thing giving *me* peace... and don't flatter yourself."

"Oh. Well, if it's not me, then you won't mind my company."

"Don't come in here."

The hand that he had reached around the curtain was suddenly pulled back.

"I wasn't coming in. I was just going to ask if you wanted to get some air, geez. Outside? Take a walk?"

"It's raining."

Rain or no rain, I was dying to take a walk outside, to stroll on the sand, listen to the waves, and even get lost in the palm trees. But I wasn't sure how that would end with Musa... Who am I kidding? I knew where it would end up with Musa.

"Life is short, Jane."

He was right about that.

"Right now, who knows how short?"

Now that was just tacky.

He tapped his fingers musically on the wall outside and waited. Finally, I threw off my blanket with a loud sigh and met him at the curtain.

"Will you put this book back in your room for me and grab a couple of flashlights?" I asked.

"Sure."

When Issa walked by and saw me slipping my shoes on, he asked,

"Where you goin'?"

"Out for a walk."

"Not alone."

"No," I agreed as Musa approached us, "not alone."

16

The name "Musa" is the Arabic equivalent of Moses. That in itself seemed pretty epic to me. Not that we were experiencing some trial of Biblical proportions or anything, but it did seem like a good sign that he was leading the way to our liberation from the rebels.

Musa had the same kind of straight forward personality as Issa. He didn't mince words and always appeared to cut to the most important aspect of a challenge. But he was witty and liked to joke around, too. I think being the oldest made him more balanced and flexible. He had an unwavering confidence, which was actually his most attractive trait to me. He also knew just when to deviate from a plan or idea. He was spontaneous at the right times, and that made him just unpredictable enough to be fun.

He was unpretentious and unapologetic in his expression of his interest in me. He didn't act like he was falling in love with me just to get into my good graces. He wasn't particularly flowery with his advances, but also wasn't disrespectful. I could have been any woman that he met one night and took a casual interest in, and that was okay. I had finally begun to understand that every romantic encounter didn't have to be burdened with an expectation of eternal commitment.

When we were far enough away from the house to feel comfortable skinny dipping, I looked at Musa and realized that none of these guys were lightweights, and that put my mind at ease even more. All of them, even Issa, had the same stocky build with beefy arms, broad shoulders and chests, and thick legs.

Musa, Jelaney, and Baturu were all around six feet tall, give or take an inch or two, while Issa carried himself like a man with tall intentions regardless of his lesser height. Their physiques had a more puffed up, rather than a ripped look. If you lined them all up, shoulder to shoulder, they'd make a pretty powerful-looking bunch. Maybe we stood a chance after all.

The drizzle on the beach increased to a moderate rain while we let go of our concerns and played in the water. Musa reminded me that it is much safer to swim parallel to the shore than to try to fight the waves head on. While he swam alongside the waves, I chose to simply float on top of them.

There was no moonlight, only millions of stars above and the light of a passing ship that revealed us momentarily. A few times, we stepped into the glow from our flashlights which were shining on the sand, and I caught glimpses of Ali in his face. No matter how far I seemed to go from that man, whether to the other side of the world or into far off dimensions in my sleep, I couldn't seem to escape the memories of him. Admittedly, it was nice to see him again there in the water.

I didn't care if a sting ray snuck up on me in the dark or if a rip current knocked me off my feet and started carrying me out to sea. It was like being a child again, back when I would poke playfully at the jellyfish swimming around my feet and never once think a fearful thought of being stung. Somehow, it seemed that giving in to that moment was the most powerful thing that we could do. There was no way we could wrestle against something as mighty as nature herself and win. Our greatest victory would come from riding the tide and using it to our advantage.

Just as the rain became a cloudburst, sending down a cascade and flashes of distant lightning, Musa pulled me close to him. The sensation of his skin against mine was consoling while the mildly scandalous mood that we were in charged this very desperate situation with some much needed humor and delight.

We smiled cheek to cheek and laughed at the apparent craziness of our playing in the ocean during a storm while on the run from a pack of murderers. Yet it all made sense and felt right—my hand in his, his lips on mine, both of us aware of but actively defying the dangers that abounded around us.

We enjoyed several moments in silence, then we heard yelling in the distance.

"It's almost here!" We heard Jelaney say as he ran toward us. "It's coming early!"

"What?" I asked, trying to hide behind Musa.

"The MV Caterina. It's arriving early, patrolling just off this coast tonight. It'll be in route to Monrovia before morning."

"How do you know?" Musa asked.

"Baturu's contact sent a messenger to tell him that they were nearing Harper. The ship just passed here. We have an hour to meet them at the Seaport." He bent over and put his hands on his knees while catching his breath but kept looking at us.

"Well, turn around!"

"Let us get dressed, man!"

Musa and I yelled at the same time, baffled by Jelaney's lack of awareness.

When we got back to the house, Fatou was packing small rations of food for us to carry. The aunties had the weapons laid out on a floor nearby along with ammunition. They immediately tried to get our attention so that they could help us decide how to negotiate boarding the ship with guns, but Musa noticed right away that Baturu and Issa were not around.

"Where are my brothers?" he asked.

The aunties slowly pointed toward the courtyard. We approached and heard yelling as we saw Issa seated in a lawn chair with his arms folded. As we walked outside, Baturu pushed past us in a rage.

"I am absolutely done with his bullshit." he said. "See if YOU two get him off his ass!"

"What's wrong?" Musa asked. Issa didn't move or say a word.

"Issa, what are you doing. We have to prepare to leave now!"

"He's on his pity pot." Baturu said. "Suddenly this is all about his him— *his* future, *his* child, *his* pretend wives—" Baturu picked up a tiny potted plant and threw it in Issa's direction. "*His* fears!"

Issa didn't flinch at the sound of the pot shattering on the ground. He only moved his head slightly to look at it after it broke, then he calmly looked at me. Musa held Baturu back as he considered coming into the courtyard again to straighten Issa out. He finally left him with,

"You have five minutes to get yourself together, little brother!"

I sat down and tried to level with him.

"What in God's name are you doing?" I asked with as much compassion as I could muster, considering the circumstances.

"I've been prayin'." he said.

"Okay."

"For the past several days, I have prayed."

"That's good."

"And it seems that God has quick timing."

"Alright, Issa—"

"I'm okay with it. I'm okay. I'm even okay with you and Musa."

"Issa, we're hardly an item. It was just—"

"Do what you want. I don't care if you sleep with my brother."

"We were just…keeping each other company."

"I don't care. Do what you want. I have my own problems."

"Issa, are you kidding me? We have got to get ready to board that ship! Will you snap out of this?"

"I have my own problems. I can forget about the bank when we go back. I have my familial obligation to my brothers and my country, I'm going to be a father soon, no one wants to marry me…"

His sulking was really getting on my nerves.

"Issa, you don't have to worry about some job. And do you really want to be married right now anyway? If you weren't prepared to propose to her before, why now? Marriage isn't going to change anything, it won't make anything better."

"...I thought I was that guy...our dad was that guy."

"This doesn't mean that you are or you aren't, but you'll have time to figure that out... You'll have plenty of time to figure that out, after all of this."

He sat up and took a deep breath.

"You have a plan. A solid one." I reassured him.

He nodded, then stood up and put his hands in his pockets while quietly staring at the trees beyond the house. Baturu stood in the doorway again and got ready to to lunge toward Issa, but I put up my hand and motioned for him to wait.

"Let's go." Issa finally said as he turned toward the house.

***

Back in the kitchen, the aunties rummaged through a couple of old plastic bags and pulled out several police uniforms. Aunt Edna went to each one of the guys, holding a uniform against them to compare sizes.

"Well," she concluded. "Your messenger only brought three uniforms, and they all fit the bigger boys."

Issa and I looked at each other.

"How are we going to board with you if we aren't in uniform, too?" Issa asked.

Musa hesitated and looked down at the ground before answering.

"Baturu and I have you covered. Don't worry."

"What does that mean?" I asked.

"We have it figured out with my contact." Baturu said while handing each of us a small handgun. "I beg, just trust us and let's get moving."

"Well, at least we'll have a good excuse for carrying weapons." Issa said to me.

The police posers got dressed in a flash and met us in front of the house. Fatou and the aunties rose to wish us well and send us off. Each of them gave each of us a hug and told us how much they looked forward to being with us again. Then, we were off into the night.

Once were out of the aunties' sight down the road, Baturu grabbed Issa and handcuffed him.

"What is this, man?" Issa yelled.

"Shh!" Baturu said. "Calm down, we need to do this to get you onboard."

"You need to start explaining very quickly whatever the hell you have planned!" Issa went on.

Musa stepped in front of both of us and told us their scheme.

"We are Liberia National Police officers." he said with surprising conviction. "You two are criminals. We've been investigating an international prostitution ring and we found you two out here, planning to lure some girls into a trafficking endeavor. We got you just in time tonight, but we need to get to Monrovia as soon as possible to hand you over to the authorities there, since that is the hub of your operations."

Musa seemed pretty proud of himself and their plan. He folded his arms and waited for our response.

"I'm a *pimp*?" Issa asked.

"You are tonight. Both of you are." Musa answered.

Issa shook his head and wiggled around the handcuffs. "Don't you need some kind of paperwork for all of this?"

"Baturu's guy has all of that covered."

"This is ridiculous!" Issa said. "What am I supposed to say if someone starts asking me stuff?"

"You're the criminal. You don't talk. Leave the talking to us. Once we're on the ship we'll stay out of sight, so there won't be much opportunity for you to run your mouth and blow our cover."

"What about her?" Issa nodded his head in my direction.

"I just told you, she's with you. You're the criminals."

"Then where are her handcuffs?" Issa asked.

"Oh, yeah." Musa pulled out another set and walked over to me.

I instinctively took a step back from him.

"I'm sorry, dear." he said. "This has to be convincing."

"We have to hurry." Baturu reminded us as his eyes scanned the road.

I looked at Issa. He only seemed partly convinced that this plan would work, but he'd stopped fighting. In the interest of time and solidarity, I gave in and held out my hands.

"I'm not letting you fasten them behind me."

I still wanted it to be relatively easy for me to use my hands if push came to shove.

"That's okay. You're a lady, so they'll be less threatened by you anyway."

He adjusted the handcuffs slowly, being sure not to hurt my arms.

"They aren't uncomfortable, are they?"

"No." I said calmly.

"Have you ever worn cuffs before?" he asked me with a little grin.

I smirked back at him but didn't answer.

"You're gonna bring this scheme to life, eh?" Baturu asked in annoyance. "Can we *go*?"

We walked for a few more minutes until we approached an empty police car parked on the side of the road.

"This is our ride." Baturu said. "Thank goodness the twelve-year-old messenger they sent to drop it off didn't crash it or get caught."

We got in and I prayed that the rain, which had stopped by now, would continue to stay away until we were off the treacherous dirt roads and at the seaport. Thankfully, that prayer was answered.

***

We stood in line waiting to board the ship. Baturu's contact, Edwin, stood in front of us explaining to a dense-looking officer who we supposedly were. He explained that he'd been given express direction from his supervisor to allow us passage and not impede the investigation that we were a part of.

"What are dese questions?" Edwin asked belligerently. "I can only confirm the order from my supervisor and the inspectors who are conducting the investigation. All other information has to remain confidential. You don want me to show myself to you-o! You can try to obstruct this process and explain for yourself to the LNP why you have refused to cooperate, or you can allow me to chunk these degenerates into holding cells immediately and allow these officers passage!"

"Holding cells?" I whispered to Issa.

Equally appalled by the notion, Issa elbowed Musa in the back.

"Pardon me. Pardon." Musa tapped Edwin on the shoulder then whispered something into his ear.

Edwin twisted his face into a look of shock and continued listening to Musa.

"Eh!" he exclaimed. Finally, he faced the officer again.

"Dese peepo are dangerous. PATICULARLY dangerous, as that briefing from my supervisor states. They cannot be simply placed in a holding cell. They must be watched."

"Watched?" The naïve officer appeared flustered and confused.

"Yes, watched! They apparently have a penchant for escape. And that woman there, bug-a-bug ate her brain. She's nah right. She has to be closely monitored to prevent erratic behavior! These men know the protocol. I suggest you promptly grant them access to one of our vacant storage cabins where they will be kept away from the ship's population."

"Eh-heh...um." The officer fiddled with the papers that Edwin had given him and almost tossed them into the air when Edwin yelled,

"Immediately!"

The officer allowed us to board and led us down a hallway just in time for us to avoid the gaze of an approaching group of UN soldiers. We settled into our cabin and ate some of the snacks that Fatou packed for us.

"So much for me being 'less of a threat' because I'm a lady." I said to Musa. "*Bug-a-bug* ate my brain?"

He laughed, "Hey, you wanna be out there in some holding cell with strange guys staring at you or safe in here with me… with us? Plus, this keeps us all out of view so people don't get suspicious."

"Yeah, okay." I said. "Hey, you know that little police officer act you put on back there was pretty convincing. Seemed like you really got into to it, like you were having fun with it."

Musa beamed. "I have a few tricks up my sleeve."

"Yeah, he's tricky alright." Issa said while busting between us to get to the other side of the room.

There was a knock at the door. We all went silent and waited, not quite knowing how to react.

"Da me, Edwin." said the voice outside the door.

We were relieved to find that it was him and not some officer or soldier making rounds or coming to give us a closer look. When we opened the door, he looked carefully to his left, then his right. He stood at the threshold with wide eyes and, in a low voice, told us that someone important needed to talk to us.

"Who is it?" Baturu asked. "We don't know anyone else here."

I think all of us were startled to learn that someone else, who we weren't aware of, knew of our presence on the ship. Edwin nodded, as if letting us know that we didn't need to be alarmed. Then he stepped aside and allowed this other person to enter the room.

The man was tall and very thin with leathery, dark skin. He appeared to be in his late sixties. He wore an impeccable navy blue suit with a white shirt, no tie, and polished black shoes. He moved slowly but, apparently, not for lack of strength or mobility. He was obviously very observant and circumspect, and was careful to give each of us a deep look in the eyes before speaking.

Finally he smiled, and Issa said, "Jajah."

This must have been the man Issa had mentioned to me a few times before, the one who had been very close friends with his father and who he always said he couldn't wait to visit again. He told me that the man was from the Kru tribe, a tribe known for their strong resistance to slave traders and their seafaring skills. It was ironic to be meeting him for the first time along the sea-going leg of our journey.

"I see you've managed to make it quite far. I knew you would." Jajah said. "Tell me, are you all well?"

"Yes, we are well." Issa answered.

"And Fatou, is she safe?"

"Thank goodness, yes."

"Jane," Jajah went on, "it is most unfortunate the way you've been caught up in this matter. I hoped my warning to you would have given you pause, but it was not enough. I am sorry. What you all must understand now is that you've reached a point of no return here. From this point forward, you are trackable. You have to stay focused on your goal and execute it quickly, without doubt or hesitation. That is your only option. I'm here to help clear the way for you."

"Wait," Musa said, "how did you find out about our plan to sail out of Harper? Could anyone else have known, too?"

"When Jelaney made the call to Edwin, he mentioned that you would need to connect with me once you reached Monrovia. Edwin and I are well acquainted since he has led security details at the AfDB office regularly for the last several years. Edwin contacted me immediately to inform me that you would need safe passage to Monrovia. I made a promise to your father, and your best interests are always in the forefront of my mind. Circumstances may require some physical distance between us, but you will always be in my care."

"Can you help us understand how we should deal with Deana?" Issa asked.

"Deana? Why would you need to deal with her here?"

"We know that she's been hiding some of her activities related to our accounts by operating through Jane's IP address at work. We think she did it to divert those rebels' attention away from herself and that she's planning to steal from us."

Jajah folded his arms. As he thought, he clinched his jaws and his forehead wrinkled, causing the skin on the rest of his face to look utterly taut.

"I think it is best for you to deal with these guys who are after you now. Whatever she is up to is most certainly related to some planned theft and it will be possible to trace her activities and provide evidence to have the authorities deal with her later."

The guys nodded in agreement, then Jajah grabbed a few papers from the inside of his jacket. We all pulled up chairs around him so we could listen to his advice for handling the rebels. We settled in and made the effort to block out the ship's ambient noise, including the hum and occasional bumps from washing machines in the laundry nearby.

First, Jajah pulled out a map of Monrovia and pointed out some areas that he had highlighted.

"The mastermind behind the kidnapping and planned execution is Fred, the man who Chike tried to kill, along with two of his comrades, Khan and Dengue."

"Just three of them now? I thought there were four." Musa said.

"The fourth fell ill and died some years ago. Thankfully, he was the one most like a brother to Fred, and he was highly passionate about this vendetta. But you have to be completely on your guard, nonetheless. Kidnapping for ransom is not new to them. It is suspected that they've been connected to several disappearances of businesspeople since the war. Somehow, though, they manage to slip out of the grasp of the authorities, likely by greasing palms."

I jumped in, "Does that mean that we also have to be concerned about these authorities that they're connected with? How many of these guys are gonna have to be knocked off before this thing is over and done with?"

Jajah gave me a curious look. "She's not the least bit nervous." he said to Issa.

Actually I was quite nervous, but fear-induced adrenaline was beginning to kick in. I was also, admittedly, feeding off my anger and desire to get revenge on Deana— whatever that revenge would be. I had that to look forward to after we took care of these rebels, even though I couldn't tell whether or not I'd sustain enough gumption to harm her physically.

Jajah continued. "No, I am certain that if you can catch them unguarded and unaware in their compound, you can defeat them and escape without any extraneous opposition. Of course, no surprise, they are junkies and drunks. Getting it done should not be very difficult if they are altered and off guard. But if they are expecting you when you show up, they will be more than ready. They know what happened in Philadelphia and that you are not as weak as they initially assumed you were."

He pointed to the map again.

"Here is their most recent compound. It's in Congo Town, not too far from the AfDB headquarters. Once you disembark from this ship, you will be escorted to a vehicle. There will be extra weapons in the trunk… including explosives."

He glanced up to see our reactions. I guess he could tell from our stillness and our undaunted expressions that we were okay with that notion. I was also glad to see that we had all fully accepted what needed to be done.

"The drive from the port to their compound should take you close to an hour. You will be monitored by two officers who I have asked to follow closely behind you. They will only become involved if there is an absolute need for them to."

He raised one finger in the air and unequivocally said, "You will completely obliterate these men. Understand? There's no going back from it."

We all nodded our heads slowly.

"I have provided you with every resource that I can. The officers that I've appointed to you will contact me if you absolutely need my assistance. Don't overthink this. The more you do, the sloppier you will become. You should rest now and be ready in twelve hours to secure your futures."

17

Twelve hours was a long time to be on a ship without any nausea medicine. It reminded me of my trip from mainland Tanzania to Zanzibar during study abroad a few years ago. There were hundreds of us packed onto the ferry. The lower deck was comfortable, but the choppy waters and the fact that the staff saw fit to play Castaway as the feature film made it less so. There was standing room only on the upper decks where people clamored to breathe fresh air. As soon as we boarded, attendants walked around with stacks of barf bags and gave each passenger one, just in case. And that was only a two-hour ride!

Since we had to stay hidden on the Caterina, we couldn't go outside to catch a breeze or stare at the horizon, which was what kept me from hurling on that ferry to Zanzibar. So, trusting that Fatou may have had the fine details of our journey in mind, I searched the bags she gave us for some stomach remedy. Sure enough, at the bottom of my bag were several long strips of fresh ginger wrapped in a piece of aluminum foil. I broke off one small piece to chew.

All the guys seemed to be doing okay except Issa. He had settled into a corner of the room for a nap but was clearly uncomfortable and holding his stomach.

"Issa. Issa, there's ginger in your bag." I said. "Why don't you try it?"

"Hmm?" He looked around for his bag and quickly dumped its contents onto the floor.

"There, it's inside the foil."

He pulled out an entire strip of ginger and balled it up.

"You may not want to use more than a piece of that. You should stretch it out. You also should be drinking a little more water."

"You know, we're gonna have to use the bathroom at some point, Jane." he said.

"We'll cross that bridge when we get to it. For now, I'd rather brave a trip to the toilet than to sit in a room with the lingering stench of vomit because you couldn't make it to one."

He broke off a small piece of ginger. I sat down next to him and looked around the room, trying to come up with some conversation to kill the time. Finally, once his chewing slowed down and he seemed a little more relaxed, I asked,

"So, you still prayin'?"

"Do I look like I been prayin'?"

I laughed. "Where is northeast from this ship, anyway?"

"Hell if I know."

"I'm sure Allah understands why you took a little break."

"Yeah, well just fill in for me, please, and ask Jesus to hook a brother up with a stronger stomach."

"You know, it's not good to go around on an empty stomach the way you do."

"It's Ramadan."

"I'm not talking about that. You do it all the time, running around on bread and water."

He tilted his head away from me, the way people do when you're saying something they don't want to hear, like their ears are trying to dodge the words.

"I thought you were trying to save money. It's not healthy."

"I eat stuff." he said dismissively.

"I know, but it doesn't seem like enough. Especially when you're studying. I know you don't cook, but clearly you have access to decent meals."

"I know. But sometimes I need to focus. Giving in to every appetite… can make a person lose focus."

I nodded in agreement, but I doubted that he sometimes avoided eating because he wanted to build mental stamina.

"Anyway…why should I live like some rich guy in America when I haven't even kept my promise to my parents and everything is still so messed up?"

"What do you mean?"

"We should have been back before now, we could have. We promised our parents we'd come back here. It was always our intention to contribute what we learned to help rebuild."

"Yeah, but it didn't seem like the right time yet, Issa. You guys needed to finish school, get some things in order. I think your parents would understand."

"We were getting comfortable," he said before bending forward with a slight leaning of the boat.

"Here," I said. "give me your arm."

I held his right hand and firmly placed my thumb on the two tendons just below his index finger. As I massaged in a circular motion, he leaned back and rested on the back of the chair again.

"I've been thinking." I said.

"About what?"

"Well… since I saved your life… and I'm technically here risking my hide to help save you again, I'ma need for you to consider breaking a sista off some compensation."

"Unbelievable." he said. "How much? What do you want, a new place?"

"Nah, bruh." I said "I'm afraid I'll need more than that. I need cash— something in the… upper thousands."

"Thousands!"

"Yeah, like HIGH thousands."

"Extortion!"

I dropped his hand in his lap, and he desperately waved it at me.

"I'm listenin'. Keep going." he said.

"See, I got the student loan mafia to pay when I get back, and they can't be gotten rid of as easily as ya'll. I am much more scared of them than I've ever been of your NPFL or ECOMOG or any African Militia Dirty Money Death Squad."

He played along with the joke and made an offer.

"Okaaaay, how 'bout twenty 'k'?"

"Tuh!"

"Fifty."

Dropping his hand for a second time, I said, "See, you know what—"

"Okay, Okay! You are gonna cost me my son's prep school education."

"I saved your son's life, too! So technically after this, ya *still* owe me. And it could be your daughter."

"I guess I'm just helping the poor and the needy." He said, leaning his head back like an addict with liquid sunshine flowing through his veins.

"Hey, if you cut me a check for a hundred thousand after all this, does that make me a hitman?"

"Ha! I don't think so. Gangsta, maybe. Not quite a hitman. But then again this conversation does constitute premeditation... ONE HUNDRED THOUSAND?" His eyes shot open.

"Just consider this reparations for what your ancestors did to mine." I concluded.

"We didn't sell you guys! We were sold as slaves, too." he snickered. "And plenty of African presidents have made public apologies for that. You're just nuts, like I said... Your mother did raise a good woman, though, however nutty."

"Yeah," I said. "You're not too bad yourself. I knew there was a good reason to keep you around."

Musa came over and observed us. "Hey, this looks very relaxing." he said.

"It's acupressure! I'm helping with his nausea."

"Looks like it's working. You are something else." He smiled and leaned forward to let me know, "I don't get sea sick, but you know that." Then he stuck a piece of calla in his mouth and strolled over to another part of the room.

Eventually, we all found comfortable spots around the room, cozied up with the blankets that Edwin gave us, and went to sleep with Jajah watching over us like an angel.

18

Our objective was to simply hide in plain sight while exiting the ship along with the slew of soldiers and police officers who temporarily disembarked in Monrovia. Edwin had managed to find police uniforms that fit Issa and me, so we no longer had to play pimp and crazy woman. The exit was surprisingly effortless, and before we knew it, we were heading away from the Freeport of Monrovia to catch the ride that Jajah had prepared for us.

In broad daylight, at eleven o'clock in the morning, the five of us set out walking down United Nations Drive donning full Liberia National Police regalia, in search of a white van accompanied by two actual LNP Officers. They were supposed to immediately recognize us, signal to us that they were in fact expecting us, and escort us to a separate, nearby vehicle which contained additional weapons. We'd drive that vehicle to the rebels' hideout in

Congo Town. The officers would follow discretely behind and cover us in the event that we needed help.

Shortly after we began walking, however, I saw a cluster of congregating police officers and realized that we were approaching the Freeport Police Station, which Jajah had expressly warned us to avoid. Hiding among transient officers on the ship was one thing, but brazenly strolling past a station where no one would recognize us could be near suicide.

"The guards that I've hired for you will be waiting about a quarter mile down the road, changing a tire as a diversion." Jajah had said. *"When you approach, they will signal to you, and you will promptly join them in the van. Do not go near that police station by the corner of United Nations Drive and Somalia Drive. If you approach the police station, you've gone too far, and you will most certainly draw unwanted attention to yourselves. DO YOU UNDERSTAND?"*

"Hold on! Something isn't right." I immediately said.

Baturu must have been thinking exactly the same thing, because, for once, he didn't hesitate to agree with me.

"Yeah, what's up? Where is this van?" he asked.

We all stopped and carefully did one full scan of the area around us.

"We definitely should have seen that van by now." I said.

"Well, we can't keep standing here or those officers down the road are going to notice us." Issa said.

"There," Musa pointed to a large grassy area behind an open gate where a couple of empty eighteen wheelers sat. "next to that hydraulics supply place. Let's go in there and call Jajah."

Everyone agreed and quickly walked through the gate. As we huddled next to it in order to make the call, a lone, elderly man shuffled out from behind one of the trucks and looked in our direction.

Musa promptly nodded to put him at ease and give him every reason to keep going wherever he was going. "Halo!" he said to the man with a wave.

The man waved, walked past us through the gate, and headed down the road without a word.

"Jajah." Issa spoke urgently into the phone. "Jajah, we have nearly approached the police station and there is no sign of the van. There are a lot of cops around and we need your help quick. We're behind the hydraulics supply place." he hung up.

"Voicemail."

Nearly ten minutes passed. Every time someone walked by in the busy, mid-weekday morning traffic, we huddled as if discussing something important and hoped the passersby were not police. We didn't want to walk any further into the surrounding grounds and risk running into any more people. Surely Jajah was scrambling to get us taken care of in this very moment.

Finally, we were all startled to see two LNP officers approach the gate. They took one look at us and quietly stepped inside.

"Jajah sent us." One of them said in a hushed tone.

"What happened to the van?" Baturu asked them.

They looked at one another then back at Baturu. "W-we had some trouble with the tire."

"Where is the van?" Baturu was quickly losing patience and was noticeably trying not to raise his voice. They turned to exit the gate, and as they gestured for us to follow them, Baturu hurried them along with, "Quickly, please, we have to move!"

We turned our backs on the police station down the street and backtracked up United Nations Drive. We didn't dare even turn around to see who may have been behind us. Within a few short moments, the two men led us off the road and into an alley where a white Winnebago sat jacked up on a tire crank with one tire lying flat next to it.

Baturu gave the officers a sharp look of disgust then knelt down to replace the tire with Musa's help. The officers tried to maintain an air of authority by standing with their arms folded and nodding periodically as the guys worked.

Jajah seemed like the kind of guy who had his stuff together, and I hoped he had taken on the right people for the job when he hired these guys to have our backs. Police officers in failed states are often underpaid and undertrained. Finding someone competent who would complete this task, remain loyal to our cause to the finish, and stay quiet about it afterwards could be a tall order. Asking that they also have the ability to quickly change a tire might be a bit much. This didn't put my mind at ease.

After the guys made short work of the tire changing, we all piled into the van and shot down Jamaica Drive.

"Where should I turn to access the second vehicle?" Baturu asked as he drove. "We should be switching cars soon, right?" The officers had not even given him the go ahead to drive. He simply took it upon himself, considering their apparent ineptness.

"It is parked along the road." One of the officers said. "We should be approaching it any minute."

"What?" Baturu asked in disbelief.

"You parked the car on the side of the road?" Issa asked. "Anyone could have seen you."

"Calm down." the officer warned Issa. "We are the officers, you are not."

"I think everybody needs to settle down." Musa said. "Yes, you are the officers, and we trust you to do what you need to do, what Jajah *paid* you to do— to protect us. I'm sure they have our vehicle waiting in a secure location." Musa assured us.

With a lowered voice, the officer agreed, "Yes. You are right... there, straight ahead, the van is right there."

Baturu squinted as another white van came into view far ahead of us.

"Right there?" he asked.

"Yes, that's it." the officer said.

Issa sat up and leaned toward Baturu. "Someone's going near it."

Baturu slowed down a little.

"They're stealing the van!" he yelled. We all watched as two young men picked the car door open, jumped into the van in a flash and started speeding off. One of the officers pushed his hands in front of Baturu and started frantically pressing on the horn.

"Ay! Stop it! Stop them!"

"What are you doing?" Baturu screamed. "You're going to draw attention to us!" He forcefully pushed the officer away from him.

"Just stay close and see what direction they head in." Musa said. "When they slow down or make a stop, we can move in."

"We're not here to chase random street thugs, Musa. We're not actual cops!" Baturu argued.

"Baturu, think, man." Musa said. "We need those weapons, and we have some time. No one knows we're here. This is a minor hiccup. The unexpected is bound to happen in a situation like this." He gave all of us a quick, reassuring look and concluded, "It's okay."

With everyone's nerves effectively calmed, we quietly followed the second van as it approached what appeared to be a settlement.

Musa poked fun at Issa who might be the least likely among them to remember his way around.

"You know where you are, baby boy?"

"Yeah," Issa responded without the least bit of enthusiasm. "Chocolate City."

"What?" I asked. "What is that, a neighborhood nickname or something?"

"No, it's the name of the place." Issa said.

"That's the nice name for it." Musa laughed.

"Huh?" I responded

"Used to be a public toilet." Baturu said sharply. He had calmed down per Musa's advice, but his patience was still thin.

Musa explained. "Used to be so bad that people passing by on the road could smell the stench."

"Oh my god!" I said. "They would just go and take dumps out in the open?"

" 'Swhat happens when you have abject poverty in a neglected pocket of town without waste treatment services." Musa responded.

"Like West Point on the other side of Monrovia." Baturu added. "They think that damn place is nature's toilet. People crap on the beach and figure the ocean will just flush it out."

"Musa, you're laughing about that? That's ridiculous." I thought it was nothing short of disgusting and utterly dehumanizing, and I had to look away from him so I couldn't see him smirk. But then I couldn't help saying, "It doesn't take government intervention for people to dispose of some things. Even animals know what to do with their own waste."

I thought of something my grandma Celia used to always say: *"Just 'cause you po' don't mean you gotta be triflin'."* For years, the woman lived in one of the most infamous housing projects in our town, but she kept her place spotless and routinely applied industrial polish to her vinyl tile floors.

Still, I knew that even the worst housing projects back in the U.S. were like community centers compared to the slums in places like this. I couldn't reconcile making such an insensitive comparison to a place that was not equipped with something as basic and essential as sewage treatment.

"Yeah, but it's not that simple, Jane. It's not just about poverty— not having resources and infrastructure. It's about poverty *mentality*. Poverty mentality and a sense of victimhood."

"How exactly does that lead to poop town?" I asked, unconvinced.

Musa went on. "Travel the world and you'll see the same kinds of problems in the slums of India, Brazil, Russia. It was the same deal in the cities in Europe and the U.S. before the industrial revolution— trash and filth everywhere, people dumping their chamber pots out of their bedroom windows and into the *streets*.

"You can burn trash, like we did with our aunties every night. You can create makeshift waste disposals, compost human waste, make fuel out if it even. Doesn't take much.

People can take it upon themselves to do those kinds of things. Indigenous people who are fully self-sufficient have done it for millennia.

"No. What the inhabitants of these slums are burdened with, along with their lack of resources, is the prevailing *idea* that they are lacking. And they want the wealthy travelers, the government officials, and the celebrities who come to film that poverty porn, to smell the stench, to see the horrible sight of these places that have been neglected."

"Even if they have to live in it?" I asked.

"I had this cat once, named Onyx." he said. "She was the most beautiful, elegant, slick black cat. Loved nothing more than for me to sit down next to her and pet her tummy. Food and petting, that was all she wanted. She was totally attached to me, but she hated leaving the house. I went out of town for a couple of days once and left her alone with plenty of food in my apartment, because I knew these jackasses wouldn't be civil enough to go and check on her." Baturu laughed as Musa punched him lightly in the arm.

"When I got back, what was it, Baturu?"

"Shit ground Zero." Baturu answered.

"My own little Chocolate City. I don't think she used that litter box once while I was gone. She wanted me to know how literally pissed she was that she felt neglected."

"Hey, they're stopping." Issa said. The second van came to a stop in a tight alley.

"I hope you guys know the way back out of here." I said.

The officers seemed eager to prove their worth after being back-seated by the guys. They both nodded to remind me that they knew the way around.

As Baturu slowly closed in behind the van, Issa asked, "So what do we do now?"

"Baturu and I, along with the officers, will approach them and get the van back." Musa said. "You three stay here and be ready to drive back out of this alley."

We sat like statues and glared at the four of them as they walked toward the van. Baturu led the way with Musa just a couple of steps behind. When they reached the van the two police officers stepped forward, each one of them approaching the front driver's side and front passenger's side windows.

They suddenly appeared shocked to find whatever was in the van. One lurched instinctively backward. The other lowered his gun slightly then took a deep breath before raising it again. They both stepped forward a second time and looked through the windows as if straining to see inside past the front seats.

They reached forward to open the front doors and out slid the limp, bloody bodies of the thieves. Each one of their throats was cut.

Then, without warning, the side door of the van flew open and out jumped one man who was dressed in all black and holding a semi-automatic rifle. Before he could lift it to pull the trigger, Musa slammed him to the ground and yanked the gun from his hands as Baturu stomped him in the stomach.

What was happening? Was this one of the rebel thugs? Had he been waiting in the van to slit *our* throats when the thieves interrupted everyone's plans? Were the officers working with him or were they just bumbling idiots?

Issa turned to open his door and leave the van, but I grabbed his arm and we both fell into shock again as another man slipped out of the back of the van. While

Musa, Baturu, and the two officers attempted to restrain the first man in black, this second one calmly walked around to where they all stood, raised a handgun, and shot Musa in the back.

Everything seemed to fall into slow motion and then froze as Musa lay motionless on the ground. Baturu didn't hesitate to charge the shooter with all his strength. They both ended up on the ground. Baturu grabbed the man's head and smashed it into the pavement as the first man in black slipped out of the officers' grip and went running down the alley. Baturu took the handgun from the other man's hand, stood above him promptly and shot him in the head.

Issa, Jelaney and I exited our van in a panic as the officers ran toward us.

"Help us get him into the van!" one of the officers instructed us. "We'll alert Jajah and get help for Musa."

"What are we gonna do?" I screamed.

Issa could only squeeze his head in anguish before helping the officers load his oldest brother's hemorrhaging body into the van. After digging wildly through the pockets of the assailant he had just finished off, Baturu stood with a small crumpled piece of paper in his hand then looked at Jelaney as if he would be the next victim.

Without saying a word, he paced toward Jelaney with a terrible scowl, then knocked him to the ground with a push.

"Get up!" he yelled mercilessly as Jelaney begged him to stop and put up his hands to shield himself from more blows.

"How much! How much did you sell us for. How much did you sell your cousin for!"

"No, no!" Jelaney screamed. "I didn't do anything like that!"

Baturu held up the piece of paper. "This note... this is your handwriting. It has our entire plan written out, from the MV Caterina to our plans to meet them in Congo Town. Who did you give it to? Why?"

"No, no, I beg! There was no malice, I swear to you."

None of Jelaney's crying was enough to convince Baturu. He pressed him against the wall with his forearm at Jelaney's throat, looked him in the eyes and said,

"I swear, I will waste your life for his. Tell me what you did!"

Tears streamed down Jelaney's face, and he gave in. "I lost it...that paper." he whimpered. "I was at that internet café. I was so sick of all the running, and fighting, and not being free, never being free. I was... just sitting there, sulking, drinking some beers... drawing on this stupid piece of paper, trying to get all this shit out my system, to wrap my mind around everything. I knew that we couldn't escape it... but I thought if I could just think it out, get it on paper and burn it or something, crumble it up and throw it into the ocean, then I could feel disconnected from it. When I left the cafe, I-I dropped it. I didn't know where. I figured it would get swept out with the trash. I tried to find it but I had to leave."

"Someone else found it for you." Baturu said. "We've been followed ever since!"

"BATURU!" Issa yelled as he grabbed Baturu's arm and wrestled with him to keep him from striking Jelaney. Jelaney hung his head in silence and shame.

Baturu yanked his arm away from Issa and stood with his nose almost touching Jelaney's. "It was your weak-minded father who got our family into this hell in the first place. I didn't think it was possible, but you are even weaker than he was."

Baturu shook his hands as if releasing a weight then warned us all, "Don't follow me."

"Baturu, where are you going," Issa pleaded.

With his back to us and the assailant's gun in hand, he responded, "To finish the job." He disappeared down the alley and left us to figure out what to do next.

The officers started up the first van and prepared to get Musa some help— if he still needed it. Issa and I gave him one last look, searching his face for any lingering signs of life and hoping for a miracle. I grabbed his hand thinking that the sense of compassion would give him some added strength to hang on with.

We couldn't waste any more time. As the van backed up leaving the three of us standing defeated in the alley, I broke down.

"Jane, you can't do this now! You hear me? Jane!" Issa held me up as sweat poured from my face, tears fell from my eyes, and my legs began to give out. "Listen, Jane, this is happening. We are in this now. You cannot lose it!"

I just shook my head. There were no words to say. This entire thing was a suicide mission. The rebel thugs, the history, this environment— this whole situation was over my head!

"Jane. Look at me." He cupped my face in his hands and spoke softly. "You are strong, and we are doing this together. There's no getting around it. You are fully capable of making it through this. It does not end here. Not now. Not today. Not here."

He was right. It couldn't be over. We had to finish what we set out to do. Issa and Jelaney both placed their shoulders under my arms and led me to the van that Jajah had prepared for our safe transit to Congo Town. The bloodstained area of the ground where Musa had been shot caught my eye as Issa started the engine. I couldn't stomach the sight of it, but I couldn't look away.

19

It was a long quiet ride to Congo Town. The mix of dreary, brick structures, concrete buildings, and clouds of red clay dust all became a blur as we rode along Somalia Drive in a daze.

At one point, Issa gently took my hand into his and held it. I appreciated his desire to comfort me and his own need for comfort. Eventually, though, I pulled away knowing that he'd need both hands to navigate through the traffic and the more sketchy patches of road.

I spoke aloud, but not to anyone in particular. "It's not fair…if Musa's dead."

It didn't matter that life was rarely fair. I still needed to say what I felt. Issa shook his head and kept silent.

"What would he have died for?" I stared out the window, knowing that I wouldn't get an answer, that there would never be a reasonable answer.

Then I remembered a quote that I had memorized several years ago in school while doing research for the Living Memorial project. It was this statement, a reflection of my deeply held spiritual beliefs, which sustained my inspiration through the entire process of designing the cemetery. The assignment had made several people in class uncomfortable, but as someone who had embraced the other side for quite some time, I understood that there was much value in life's cycles— however cruel and unrelenting.

"Sometimes death is the only path to life." I said softly, attempting to further soothe myself and make sense of the situation. I heard Jelaney sigh and could feel his discomfort with my words, but they needed to be said. I repeated them once more. "Sometimes death... is the only path to life."

***

We arrived in Congo Town at midday. Issa pulled out Jajah's map in order to pinpoint the exact location of the hideout, then he continued driving for several minutes. Soon, we spotted our destination, which was surprisingly easy to find. After exiting Somalia Drive— which was a fairly large highway— onto a narrower street, we took a couple of left turns and we were there. I could smell the seawater nearby.

"We're near the ocean again." I said.

Issa nodded.

From outside, the place appeared to be a well-maintained, suburban house. Issa told me that it had once been a nice bed and breakfast. The thugs had most certainly shaken down the previous owners and taken it as their own.

We sat a ways up the road, under the cover of a dense patch of brush, watching the house and the activity going in and out. I was immediately jolted by the sight of Deana as she stood just outside the compound wall talking to another gun-toting man who was dressed in all black, similar to the guys who ambushed us in the alley.

"There she is." I said to Issa. "Not only is she gonna throw us to the wolves. She's housing them in her own lair and planning to feed us to them by hand."

My eyes locked onto her like a stalking animal. The hairs on the back of my neck stood up and a chill shot through my spine causing me to shudder. I could feel my jaw tingling as my teeth clamped down on each other, the way they do whenever I have that recurring nightmare about breaking free from Jack's oppressive grip and sending him over that cliff in Bermuda to his death.

The taste of blood filled my mouth before I even realized I was breaking the skin of the insides of my cheeks. Fear could have forced me into a trembling fit if I had not been suddenly overcome with a surprising sense of anticipation.

If death was the only way there was, then I wouldn't fear it. I would use it to my advantage. I would welcome, even relish it. I would throw a leash around its neck and walk it right through those doors to meet Deana.

I faded in and out of attentiveness as Issa talked gently to Jelaney, encouraging him to look ahead, to be strong for this last leg of our mission. He assured Jelaney that they were family no matter what, like brothers. He mentioned something about forgiveness in the spirit of Ramadan.

Then he told both of us about how we could accomplish our task in the least amount of time.

Wait until nightfall... catch them off guard... something about two pipe bombs and a rocket launcher in the back of the van... assault rifles... knives for keeping things quiet when we didn't want to be heard... if we have to separate, meet up again here or there in this much time... take out the guys in black first and fast.

We sat sweating through the heat, taking inventory of the weapons and rehearsing scenarios, nibbling through the last bits of food that Fatou packed for us. We dozed off in rounds. At last, it was time to move.

We alerted Jajah by text message that we were preparing to enter the compound, but he didn't respond. There was no way to know if he would be able to get us any additional backup in time.

As we stalked the grounds outside the compound gate, we heard men's voices laughing and joking before they stepped outside. Issa moved forward in a flash and knocked one of them in the face with the butt of his rifle. Before the second man knew what hit him, Jelaney followed up with a blow to his face. Issa and Jelaney looked at each other stunned and knowing what had to be done next if we were going to proceed in the manner that Jajah had advised.

But they couldn't do it. I could tell that after everything, they still weren't ready. And there was no time for uncertainty, no room for error. I grabbed the knife from the holster that Issa had attached to his belt and, without thinking any further, knelt over the first man.

I bowed my head in remembrance of the lesson I'd learned about death and prepared to do what had to be done with an abrupt slicing of his neck. Then there were more footsteps from the opposite side of the gate. We all panicked and ran around to the side of the house, hoping that whoever was walking around would not venture outside the gate and see the unconscious men before we could do some real damage inside.

As we scrambled to find a way inside, I felt an internal conflict brewing, but not one that I would have expected. It had been surprisingly easy to kneel over that man in preparation for his slaughter.

I thought, *"Shouldn't I feel shaken by what I was getting ready to do? Where's the God in me, where's the guilt?"*

Why wasn't I inclined to hesitate the way Issa and Jelaney had? Where was the anguish of wrestling with the thought of being party to another person's demise? Who were these men, anyway? Who were their wives, their children? What else had they done?

Where were my inner voices who so often tried to talk sense into me regarding matters much less important than this? Was I too hyped up on adrenaline? In my prime god-fearing days, I had felt more guilt for lusting after guys in magazines!

"Some things need getting rid of."

This was something even my loving, devout mother always said. She said it about pedophiles and the kinds of sickos who couldn't be stopped or reformed despite all the insight humanity has been able to muster so far. Warlords and their henchmen could be included in that bunch. They were the worst of the worst for sure.

Things were transpiring so fast that I didn't have time to stop and deeply consider the moralism of it all. Or maybe I just stopped caring. Though I didn't want to acknowledge it, with every enemy down, I felt I was gaining something. It was something palpable, like a quickening.

I felt it when the lead kidnapper stood before me with eyes bugged and my bullet passing through his chest. I felt it again as that guy in black let out a gust of breath as Baturu smashed his head into the ground.

Honestly, I even felt it the moment Jack died. When his glossy eyes stared up into heaven from the dark water's surface as Ali and I stood triumphant on that cliff back in Bermuda, I felt strong.

I felt my heart grow, as if a new pint of fresh, pristine blood pumped through my veins with the defeat of every person who tried to defeat us. I had never been anything close to a hunter, but now I understood the exhilaration.

Not wanting to take any chances, we moved silently through the house, carefully searching each room. I reached an upstairs bedroom where Deana sat at a gilded vanity, preparing for what she must have thought would be a lovely evening. She slowly combed her hair and basked in fragrant lavender incense as the scent filled the room, seeping into the silky sheets on her bed, a large shaggy carpet, and the posh curtains at the oversized windows.

She looked down to enjoy a series of text messages sent to her phone. Even with my reflection in the mirror which sat directly in front of her, she had no idea I was in the room until the barrel of my revolver was pressed against the back of her head. I let her turn around to face me then knocked her to the ground with one blow.

"Scream and you lose one hand. Try to fight me and you lose both."

Killing her immediately didn't seem like justice considering the kinds of people she was in cahoots with. I gave her a moment to catch her breath, but wasn't planning to give her much longer.

Finally, she raised her hands cautiously and knelt in front of me. Her eyes raced back and forth from the gun to my face. I held my hands tightly together to keep the trembling hidden.

"Stay there." I sat down on the bed and stared back at her.

"What is it with you, huh?" I asked. "Your privilege isn't enough? Your Mercedes, your condo in the city, your prestigious degrees and your great job. None of that was enough?"

Her eyes searched mine as if she was questioning me back.

"Wasn't it you going on and on just a couple of months ago about your family's annual vacations in Martha's Vineyard, about your cotillions. Didn't you *just* shove your phone in my face for ten whole minutes telling me about that stupid, three-thousand-dollar dress your mom made you wear to the opera when you were sixteen, which you hated because it wasn't the Vera Wang you wanted? I don't get it."

She sighed in annoyance and tried to regain some control of the situation. "Jane, I can expla—"

"Don't talk to me. Don't say my name. You don't know me. You don't know anything about me... but you were going to have me killed. You had no problem with the idea of disposing of me and my friends. Thought you could just pin all your shady dealings on the clueless secretary."

I stood up and checked the revolver's chamber to see how many bullets I had available. I could tell I was making her nervous. Part of me wanted her to lunge forward and give me a reason to shoot her. The longer I stayed there, letting out my anger, the less this felt like self-defense, and the more I became acclimated to my rage.

"What are you doing?" Deana finally blurted out. I didn't answer. "You gonna keep pacing around the room talking about my wonderful life?"

She stared hatefully at me as I rummaged through her makeup and clothes, throwing them around the room in my wake.

"It wasn't personal, okay?" she went on. "You don't get it. People like you never get it. You just grind away at the hamster wheel every day, working your life away, doing what everyone says you're supposed to do. And then you end up broke, in a shitty life with nothing to show for all your hard work and morals!

"You think I have privilege? I do. My family members were among the people who built this nation, and they knew there was nothing poor about Liberia. When the war tried to take everything my family established, took my extended family, my cousins, their children...I knew how to get something back.

"What did you see when you got here? Did your bleeding heart see poverty, the sad aftermath of war, your noble friends who want to piece their homeland back together one raggedy community effort at a time? I saw diamonds, investment opportunities, relationships with powerful people. Not *good* people, Jane. Powerful people. *That's* what matters. My life is wonderful.

"So, sorry. You can do what you want to me if you think you have the guts, but it won't get you anywhere.

You don't have what it takes to be me or anyone like me. Your chances of success plummeted the day you were born."

Though I remained visibly undaunted, I had felt an angry heat rise all the way up through the top of my head as she spoke. It burned through the anxious nausea in the pit of my stomach, seemingly snuffed out the relentless vibration of my heart and shaky hands, and shot right out of my eyes as I knelt next to her with one hand on the back of the empty vanity chair.

"You're right." I said with a renewed sense of calm. "I'm definitely not like you. But here's how. When I wanna screw someone over... I don't beat around the bush."

In a motion so fast and fluid it almost felt like it came from something outside me, I lifted the vanity chair and struck Deana with it. Her head flung backward and hit the floor, knocking her unconscious. I was hardly through with her. I sat down in the chair and waited for her to come to.

***

Deana was still out cold when I heard someone approaching the bedroom door. Maybe it was the guys coming to let me know the coast was clear. I was relieved as Issa appeared in the doorway, but then I saw that he was being escorted by someone who had an arm wrapped around his neck and a gun to his face. It was one of the guys that we knocked out on the way into the house. When the second man busted into the room and charged toward me, I had no choice but to put down my weapon.

Three men led Issa, Jelaney, and me down to the large living room where three full-sized, tan, leather sofas sat in a u-shape. Their inside backs and arms were inlaid with polished wood. They reminded me of the gorgeous sofas that I'd seen sitting in dusty, roadside yards outside the furniture markets of Dar es Salaam, their makers crouching next to them giving each piece a final shine. The skillfully carved sofa legs looked like swirling, oversized antlers chopped off at their thickest sections.

These works of undeniable craftsmanship were set among all manner of glitzy, tacky, and downright cheap, Italian-import-style tables, lamps and accessories. There were at least two of each furniture item, even the huge glass and gold-colored metal entertainment center that housed an array of animal knick-knacks. Two lion skin rugs sprawled across the cool, tiled floor with the same entitled laziness that they might have enjoyed just after a kill somewhere in the Eastern or Southern African grasslands.

Art filled the walls, from just beneath the ceilings down to the floors. There were Tinga-Tinga paintings, framed Indigo and Dogon cloths, and photographs of Kalahari bushmen, West African Kings, and the pyramids of Sudan. Then there was the taxidermy— at least twenty different animal heads, from aardvarks to zebras, mountain lions to the classic moose. It was an eclectic but primarily afro-chic décor that screamed conspicuous consumption and made me want to vomit.

But there was something else turning my stomach— a vivid stench of sewage, stagnant mud and rotten meat that seemed completely out of place until I zeroed in on something between two of the couches.

A man was seated on the middle sofa facing us. He calmly brushed condensed droplets from a bright green beer bottle with a red, white, and gold label that boldly read "Club Beer". Surprisingly, he didn't look much older than us. He was slim with a crisp fade and baby dreads. I could tell he was medium height, definitely not as big as our guys. He wore black jeans with a designer hoodie and like new sneakers along with gold rimmed shades. He smiled from ear to ear the moment we approached and stroked the head of a chained hyena which rested on its hind legs directly to his left. This animal, his pet and tool of terror, was the source of the god-awful stink.

A little further to his left, on the next sofa, sat Fatou, frozen and trying to hide the fear in her eyes. When Issa saw her, he immediately started wrestling with the man who restrained him, to no avail. The man on the couch seemed amused by Issa's struggling, but finally raised his hand to get everyone's attention.

"Hey! Hey, stop dis nonsense!"

"Who are you?" Issa hissed. The hyena stood up and stared at Issa, but the man coaxed it back down with a shake of the chain.

"Slow down." the man responded. "Don't look to me like you have anywhere to go. I was just gonna tell you, dammit. You shouldn't be expectin' some kind of hospitality. Dis place that you took it upon yourselves to barge into belongs to me, Frederick Douglas, and I don't suffer intruders gladly. You dingos should know dat well."

At the sound of that ethnic slur reserved for Mandingoes, Issa slung a fist in Frederick's direction and spat toward him. That only made the bully laugh. He leaned forward to place his beer on the coffee table then continued,

"I'll introduce my good friends, who I know you been dyin' to meet. Dengue and Genghis Khan." He pointed to both men as they emerged from opposite sides of the room. These must have been the two remaining masterminds behind the scheme to kill the guys and steal their money.

If the situation had not been so perilous, I might have laughed upon hearing those ridiculous names. The names, which they had clearly not been born with, were a reflection of their time as soldiers during the war. During that time, warlords adopted names that were supposed to indicate their deadliness, egomania, or sheer craziness, and strike fear into the hearts of anyone who heard of them.

Apparently, Frederick still fancied himself some kind of freedom fighter. Among many others, there had been General Mosquito of Sierra Leone, whose name brought to mind the disease carrying, death-dealing nature of the bug. There was General Mosquito Spray who vowed to take out General Mosquito as swiftly as, say, a can of OFF!. And there was the notorious General Butt Naked whose reign involved human sacrifice, hard drug use, and going into battle nude. He led a unit of cannibal child soldiers known as the Butt Naked Brigade who routinely drank their victim's blood, but he later found Jesus and became an evangelist. Seriously.

Dengue and Genghis Khan sat down on the remaining couches. They wore the same kind of shades that Frederick donned, which didn't do a good job of covering up a horrible forehead-to-chin scar on Dengue's face. He looked like he was starving and moved slowly like he was in some kind of daze, but he kept his attention on the situation at hand. For all intents and purposes, he looked like an embodiment of the disease he was named after. He was probably high on drugs, just like Jajah said.

Khan, on the other hand, looked like the most sober of them all. He was also the biggest, with muscles so pronounced his clothes seemed almost too little and an awkward posture that made him look like he was having a hard time maneuvering around his own body. He didn't say anything. He just took off his glasses and sat with his elbows on his thighs and his hands folded in front of him while he looked ahead, expressionless.

Continuing at a slower pace and with a less angry tone, Frederick slurred,

"Dengue here is my computer whiz. He got most of da information we needed about da money, but he needed some help gettin' under Deana's skin. Dat's where I come in, cuz you can see I'm da diplomatic one. Khan handles da security leg of our operation. Helps us whip our little army of rebels into shape whenever we on a mission. Plus he did some studyin', so he knows plenty book. Now, don't waste your time tryin' to outsmart us."

Khan looked at us for the first time. Prior to adding his two cents he had acted as if we were not even worthy of a glance. When he spoke, the low bass in his voice almost shook the room.

"I am not at all pleased with what you did to my special forces unit in Philadelphia, but I have to say, they turned out to be pretty useless. I promise, you won't get away so easily this time."

"The war is over and done with." Issa declared. "The people have reconciled and moved on. You guys are still running around with these cartoon names, preferring war over peace?"

"Nothing has *ended*, Issa." Frederick said. "People may be tired of fighting, but dey still want what's due them. Me, I been fighting for da liberation of my people since I was thirteen. It has to continue, somehow, 'til there's real victory."

"Bullshit!" Issa blurted out. "You're no political idealist. You're just another opportunistic moron sweeping up crumbs of power!"

Dengue and Khan remained unbothered while Frederick feigned surprise with a gasp.

He sucked his teeth and shouted "Ask Fatou! She knows what kind of soldier I am! She trained wit me, and she would have been one of our best fighters— our own Colonel Black Diamond— if dose boys from da UN hadn't stolen her from me."

Issa didn't appear surprised to hear about Fatou's previous time with Charles Taylor's army, but it was a jarring revelation for me.

"We were pretty close back then." he said. He paused and gave Fatou a serious look. "We shared a lot. But, apparently, everything's different now."

The scruffy hyena rose clumsily to its feet as Frederick suddenly became energized and stood up. He stretched backward then sprang forward to balance himself. He paced in front of us, dragging the chain back and forth while the animal sat sniffing in our direction.

"You started a family! You've lived your life abroad, been educated in da States, and started a family. You real coloh bois." He shook his head with an expression of genuine amazement. "Dat is definitely some progress. I'm jealous! You and your brothers have such bright futures ahead of you— except dat *dead* one."

Issa and I quickly cut our eyes at each other. The mention of Musa stung to my core, and I could only imagine what it did to Issa. In spite of that, we held our own and remained steady in the faces of our enemies.

Frederick stopped pacing and did another dopey drunk dance to gain a firm footing, swaying gently from side to side. Then he made a suggestion. "I'm only thirty. Perhaps we should all trade places. I and my people can fly over to da land of milk and honey, knock up a few girls and live under a cool black president— one who isn't a despot. And you guys can stay here."

He looked at Issa and Jelaney as if he actually expected an answer. "Would that be a fair trade? I get da millions, of course. I'll take my old friend Fatou wit me. You can hold fort here. And you can keep dat other one dere, dat skinny, half-breed, slave nigga you dragged out here."

I wasn't sure I was hearing him right.

"Half-breed slave nigga?" I thought. *"Does he own a mirror?"*

I was well aware of the wide cultural, spiritual and social divides that separated Black Africans, Diasporan Black Africans and their descendants. Those divides were rooted partly in the plague of white supremacy and partly in the same tribalistic nature that had afflicted the human race since time immemorial. I knew that African Americans were often held in the lowest regard by some of us, but I had chosen to believe that such a moronic view was the exception rather than the rule. It had never stared me in the face and dared to speak its mind.

I was much more amused by his comment than concerned about any misinformed opinion he may have of me. And ultimately, I had to remember that these pissing contests between bloodlines were in large part to blame for the horrendous war and this disaster that I had found myself smack dab in the middle of.

Frederick barely looked at me sideways then taunted me for the long locs that I wore.

"RASTAAAA!" He shouted at me, leaning back in another drunken swoon. "Eh, you rasta? Rastas be dry like dat." he said to Dengue and Khan, assuming that I would take his mentioning of my "dryness", or thinness, as some putdown.

Issa stood silently grinding his teeth and, no doubt, waiting for just the right moment to strike out again. Frederick stared into his eyes, mocking him. Pretty soon, the two men were seething, toe to toe. The hyena sensed the tension and threatened Issa by jumping toward him over and over, only to be yanked back by Frederick's chain just in time. The stink of it made Jelaney heave.

"Don't worry, " Frederick said, "I won't un-muzzle him yet!"

Dengue and Khan suddenly became animated as they erupted into laughter along with Frederick. They had a good, stomach-crunching, knee-slapping laugh at our expense. Whenever Dengue was able to catch his breath, he repeated "Rasta!" as if it was the funniest thing he'd ever heard. Khan stoked him by gesturing with his hand as if he was smoking a joint.

"Where are our aunties?" cried a shaky voice that was nearly unfamiliar by now. It was strange to hear Jelaney pipe up in the middle of this rough scene. He had almost not spoken at all since Musa got shot and Baturu stormed off to who knows where. He had proven himself to be our group's weakest link, but he hadn't given up. Oddly, now, he seemed to be gaining courage.

"Your *aunties*?" Frederick asked. "Oh, the ones you hid out with on the beach in Harper at dat nice blue house?" He paused while we waited in terrible suspense for an answer. Then he finally said, "We don't know. Dey must have been out preaching or buying hens or whatever a couple of old ladies do when we found Fatou. I have to say, I totally didn't think you guys would have the balls to come back here. When we found out about what you were doing, we were thrown for a loop. But while we waited for you to show up, Dengue figured out a way to get into your Cayman accounts— da ones you tried to pretend were Swiss to throw us off. So, da process of getting information from you isn't going to have to get as messy as we first planned. You should be glad about dat. We'll all just have a quick going away party and be out."

He knelt down next to the hyena and gently petted its back. "And you guys won't have to worry about what's on da menu." he said to it. "You and your friends have got a real delicacy coming your way."

20

Now finished with his introduction, Frederick roamed over to the windows that overlooked the back of the compound. As he pulled open the tall, black velvet curtains, light bulbs hanging from a few dangling wires revealed a grassy backyard. They made it easy to see four more hyenas out there lazing around while chained to stakes in the ground. They all went into a laughing and running fit when someone stepped quickly into the backyard to throw some hunks of bloody meat at them. It seemed like only an appetizer, though, just a few scraps meant to get them riled up and wanting more.

The henchmen who had brought us before Frederick, Dengue and Khan gripped us more firmly in order to haul us off to our fate. Issa and Jelaney tried again to fight them while I was simply too stunned by the thought of our impending demise to move.

It felt like we were already dying, drowning in the ear-splitting laughter of these beasts. The hyenas along with our captors all belted out deafening cackles in an array of pitches and speeds. It was a swarm of hellish noise— like dogs barking and nails scraping chalk boards, and glass shattering, and trapped souls screaming. It seemed there could be no other, more all-encompassing sound which could drown it out.

But then, we heard a rapid and powerful melody that rang out like singing angels. It was a chorus of machine gunfire that whizzed through the backyard, striking every one of those wild, dirty beasts. Frederick screeched in tune with the mayhem as he stood by and watched all of his prized animals being murdered so quickly and so mercilessly.

Dengue and Khan ripped through the living room and headed for the door to the backyard. Just before they reached it, it was blown to dust and they were both knocked out by the explosion. Standing just on the other side of that smoky, gaping doorway was Baturu, who didn't hesitate to step inside and empty a round into the two unconscious men.

Just as the guys who restrained us raised their weapons, Jajah entered directly behind Baturu and shot Jelaney's captor in the head. For some reason the other two hesitated, probably from the shock of witnessing such a rapid turn of events. With Baturu, Jajah and Jelaney all pointing guns in their directions, they released Issa and me, lowered their weapons and began begging for their lives.

"It's a little too late for mercy." Jajah said. Then he shot each one of them in the chest, in keeping with his own word.

The five of us moved through the house looking for Frederick, who'd slipped away with Fatou in the midst of the chaos. Baturu made quick work of barricading the gate in front and shooting out the tires on all the vehicles except ours. Back inside, the silence only grew as we stalked Frederick. The only sounds were the shuffling of our own feet and a few intermittent cackles from that one remaining hyena.

Baturu and Jelaney covered the first level of the house while Issa, Jajah, and I went upstairs. The first room that we encountered was that same bedroom I was in before. Except this time, Deana was sprawled out on the floor dead with a gunshot wound to the head.

"Who did this?" I asked Jajah. "Did you guys do this?"

"No." he responded. "Frederick isn't wasting any time removing dead weight. Probably knew she would've had him killed the first chance she got. There's no honor among thieves."

While Jajah and I inspected that room more closely, Issa drifted off down the hall, anxious to find Fatou. Then, I heard a chuckle right behind me. Standing in the doorway was the last spotted hyena without its muzzle.

He bounded into the room. Jajah jumped in front of me and held out his right arm. The animal clamped down on his hand with seeming delight. I ran around the room to get a clear shot of it and, to my astonishment, it released Jajah before I could fire. It turned and looked at me.

"Greedy bastard!" Jajah shouted while trying to use his weapon with his shredded hand. "It can't decide which one of us to eat first!"

"Move!" I shouted.

With Jajah out of the way, I fired one shot and grazed the animal's side. I fired two more shots and fell to the ground as it came straight at me and slammed into the wall next to the bedroom door. It stood again quickly and leapt into the air with a final giggle before a single bullet struck the side of its head.

"I thought they were supposed to be scavengers." Issa said after firing the kill shot. He helped me to my feet.

"Yeah," I said, "I wouldn't have minded if he had chosen to dine on Deana's carcass over there."

Baturu and Jelaney, drawn upstairs by the barrage of gunfire, stumbled into the room and asked if we were okay. Jelaney shook a pillowcase loose and wrapped it around Jajah's hand.

Baturu looked out the window and shouted, "There!"

We all looked down and saw Frederick sneaking out of the house, literally dragging Fatou with him. She had broken out of her fearful stupor and was fighting with all her might to get away from him. Baturu and Issa bolted down the stairs, but Jelaney went running in the other direction, toward the back of the house.

"Come on!" Baturu screamed at him. "What are you doing back there? Let's go!"

When we made it to the front yard, Frederick was frantically looking over several of the cars and realizing that they were not drivable. Then he started shooting in our direction as we ducked behind one of the disabled trucks.

A fatigued Jajah tried his best to shoot him while still perched in the bedroom window, but he missed. Frederick held Fatou close and shot back at the bedroom window while making sure that it was still too risky for any of us to shoot in his direction.

But as Fatou ducked to avoid being caught in any crossfire from above, Jelaney appeared from behind

Frederick's car, as if materializing from nothing. He held a machete from the weapons stash in the van Jajah had prepared. His head slightly down, he took several stealthy steps forward and fixed his focus on Frederick like there was nothing else in the world happening in that moment. Then he whipped the machete into the air and back down in one quick and fluid motion. He grabbed Fatou and ran out of sight behind the house as Frederick collapsed onto the car in agony, the wound on his lower leg drenching his foot and the ground beneath it with blood.

Frederick grabbed his gun and slithered behind his car, even as he was inundated with gunfire. Issa, Baturu, and I tried to finish him off in the dark fog of dust and chaos. We knew at least one of our bullets hit him after he hit the ground. Before he took refuge behind the battered car, we saw the red droplets spray like shattered glass into the air and shimmer in the yellow haze from streetlights.

For several moments, there was silence. A low thunder rumbled through the air followed by distance sparks of lightning. A curtain of mist fell upon us and quickly turned into a full on ablution. Was this finally the end?

An eerie, high-pitched sound pierced the air, as if another one of those dreaded hyenas was still on the loose. It was Frederick. He chuckled once, then again. He giggled a little louder. Finally he burst into full-blown laughter punctuated by labored breaths. With every second that he paused to take in some desperately needed air, he gasped and sounded like he would break down into tears.

"Shit! I thought I had you… but you beat my time! I don't believe it! Can you all believe this? All these years… and you come here and destroy it in a few days? Ha! What is this? If only the war had ended this quickly… You men should have been soldiers!"

"Is he cracking up?" Issa asked in amazement.

"No." Baturu said. He reloaded his handgun and poised himself to take another shot from behind the truck. "He's just cornered and trying to throw us off."

"I... uh... I think I may have gotten dis whole thing wrong-o. What has all of dis fighting brought us to, eh? I-I've been fighting since I was a child. It's all I've known."

"Don't listen to him." Jajah said as he shuffled around to where we were hiding. "Do not let up until this is finished."

"But...maybe it's already finished." Issa said.

"Issa." Baturu said his name in an effort to reel him back in from this sudden lapse into remorse.

"Did those few moments of silence distract you, son?" Jajah asked. "What are you saying?"

"Maybe it's not necessary to kill any more. Maybe, in this moment he has seen the error of his ways."

"Issa!" Baturu said in frustration.

"If nations can reconcile, why can't we at least find some way to stop killing? What if mercy is required here?"

"Now is not the time, little brother! Reconciliation happens after weapons are relinquished, NOT on the battlefield!"

"I can't do it. Add more blood to our hands. When will it stop?"

"It will stop when we no longer have to live on the run!"

"Look at him. He's just like us!"

"He's not at all like us!"

As the brothers bickered I looked toward Frederick and saw him struggle to his feet. He steadied himself then slowly lifted a Rocket Propelled Grenade Launcher up past his hip. In seconds he would be hoisting it onto his shoulder and pointing it in our direction. This was certainly no time for remorse on our parts.

As we all stood to run for our lives, Frederick fumbled with the weapon, since his drunkenness still hadn't quite worn off. We looked toward the gate which Baturu had barricaded.

I looked back at the house. There were two figures standing on the roof. It was Fatou and Jelaney. Jelaney caught his breath while Fatou stood fixated on the madman.

A brooding was in her eyes, as if the spirit of one of those frozen predators had leapt off the living room wall, jumped into her skin, and zeroed in on Frederick, her prey. In the wet, sea salty night, the skin of her neck and shoulders glistened and trapped the glow from the streetlight. Her red tank top and fitted blue, fashion jeans were stained with Frederick's blood, as if he had marked her as his... or vice versa.

She touched the trigger and peered through the scope of a second RPG. Jelaney, standing nearly two heads above her, waved quickly toward the side of the house, signaling for us to keep it moving as we filed out from behind the truck and made our escape.

Once we reached the side of the house, I could see Jelaney on the roof just above us. He waved to Fatou, and we all fell to ground and covered our heads.

When that RPG unleashed its grenade, causing it to detonate on contact with Frederick's car, I was deathly afraid that we had not run far enough. The shock wave that pulsed through the ground and our bodies was so intense, I thought it would strike the house and make it collapse right on us.

In an instant, Baturu was leading us back onto our feet and toward our van just outside the gate.

After we slammed the side door of the van shut, it was yanked open again. Issa and I drew our weapons with lightning speed but lowered them immediately when we saw that it was Fatou and Jelaney who had safely escaped the roof of the house.

Fatou glared at each of us as if taking a head count, then, with a deep sigh, nodded her head slowly. We knew then, that our task had been completed.

21

We skidded away from the house, through a web of back streets and onto the main road. The onslaught of monsoon rain battered the windshield and made the road ahead look like a red river. Somehow we avoided being tossed by or trapped in the many craters that lay just beneath the water. Maybe it was our prayers that kept us. After making my appeal to God, I could hear Issa reciting his own:

"Rabbi anzilni munzalan mubarakan wa anta khairul-munzileen."

I had heard this prayer several times before while traveling through Zanzibar and remembered that it meant: *"Oh, Lord, let me land at a blessed landing place, and You are the best to accommodate us."*

Once we hit a less treacherous stretch of road and Baturu was able to devote a little attention to forming words, he braced himself to ask the question that was likely on all of our minds.

"So, what happens next for our brother?"

Jajah turned toward him and asked. "What do you all think would be best for him?"

"Well," Baturu answered,"...the only family that we have here are the aunties... We have friends and some cousins in the States. Everybody else is in Nigeria. He would want to be here."

Issa spoke up, but I could see he was fighting through a desire to remain silent. The words seemed to hurt him as they came out.

"Yeah. And taking him back... to the U.S. ... wouldn't work, considering the circumstances."

"Try and rest your minds." Jajah said. "All will be taken care of. It's too soon for you to try and sort this out. Trust me. Rest now."

With Jajah's direction, Baturu drove through the night into more countryside, dodging potholes and a couple of clusters of parked police officers. They stood next to roads, drinking sodas and talking casually as if an insurgency had not just occurred a few miles away, or as if such an aftershock was simply mundane.

Deeper into the greenish black, we approached a private, unmarked landing strip surrounded by brush and trees. We saw a man waving at us. He looked very familiar.

"Is that Sebastien?" I asked.

"Yes it is." Jajah said. "He's proven himself to be a trusty pilot, yes?"

We all got out of the van to meet Sebastian while two men in what looked like white doctor's coats scurried around a nearby sedan. One of them gathered up some bags and boarded the plane. The other appeared to be breaking down a small, makeshift medical tent and placing its parts into the car.

"You expecting more trouble?" Baturu asked Jajah.

Jajah stopped in front of us and turned around with a serene grin.

"No. Not at all." he said. He started walking briskly toward the plane again and waved for us to follow him. "We'll go to my place in Cabo Verde. You can decide what to do next after you've had some time to rest there."

"What about our Aunties?" Issa asked.

"They're fine, I assure you. You'll see them soon."

Jajah stood next to the aircraft with his hands resting peacefully front of him, despite his injury. He reminded me of a funeral director, the way he just stood by with compassion and patience as we advanced in our solemn procession. He waited for all of us to board before entering behind us. He assured each of us with a loving smile, a gentle squeeze of the shoulder, some encouraging words. It helped. He was giving us a soft place to land after an unimaginable trauma, and I was grateful that someone among us still had the strength to be optimistic of the future.

We were each so entranced by our own sadness and exhaustion that we barely noticed that there was someone sitting under a blanket in the very last seat in the plane's rear. Just before we were all settled in our seats, we heard a murmur from that direction,

"Are you serious? I'm so dead to you, you don't even see me?"

We turned sharply to take a second look.

"Goddammit, Musa!" Baturu yelled as he jumped up to embrace him.

"Hug me, don't kill me! I just came *back* from the dead."

Issa almost fell to the floor in laughter and amazement. We all absorbed the moment in awe. Everyone took turns greeting him as if he really had returned from the dead and might evaporate back into oblivion if we weren't careful to hold him tight and make sure he was definitely there. So what if it hurt him a little— he'd get over it.

He noticed me nervously staring at the sling and bandages which covered his right arm, shoulder, and head. Thank God none of that handsome face was damaged beyond repair!

He explained, "No arteries or bones. Straight through the muscle right here near my neck. It was hitting the ground that knocked me out."

The guys kept doting on him, asking how comfortable he was and if the medical care he'd received so far was adequate. He had everything he needed but would need to follow up with a trusted physician in Cabo Verde once we arrived.

Baturu prodded Jajah for an explanation of why he'd gone so long without telling everyone that Musa was still alive.

"He was immediately taken to the doctors. When I heard of what happened, I left my office to find you and help the others. With all that transpired, I hadn't gotten any word on his condition until just before we arrived here."

Jajah stood in the middle of the aisle with all of us looking on like he was a storyteller sharing a wild, exciting tale of an adventure that we had not just lived.

"First, I was tempted to go back to that area in Chocolate City where Musa was shot, but I knew Baturu would be far from there by then. Everyone would have to meet back at Frederick's compound eventually, so I set out to go there. I caught up with Baturu on Somalia Avenue, heading down the road like a bull dog after sniffing out that goon. I think he had gotten desperate enough to consider stealing a car for quicker travel, because when I saw him, he was reaching for his weapon and slowly approaching some sleepy delivery guy in a truck."

"Thank goodness you didn't have to see that play out." Issa said.

Baturu defended himself. "I wouldn't have hurt the man, but the mission was the mission."

Fatou stood next to me and tried to be discrete while elbowing me in the side and pointing to Musa. I was the only one who had sunken into the background and wasn't really talking to him. For the most part, I still felt like an outsider who shouldn't interfere with such a profound moment for the family. I'd talk to him, but I rationalized that his brothers should have their chance first.

"Shh. Shhhhh." I insisted while she kept trying to push me to do something warm and fuzzy.

Soon the guys noticed and stared at us. I have never been a big public displays of affection kind of girl.

"Um…I'm really glad to see you're okay, Musa." I said sincerely. "I—"

O Jesus, were those tears forming in my eyes, again?

"I'm just really glad that you… that everyone's okay."

I wanted the spotlight off me, and quick. We had just dodged being kidnapped by warlords, eaten by hyenas, and blasted into infinity. I had no interest in putting on a show. Once we were a little more settled in and things were quieter, perhaps later in the flight when we had some privacy as everyone else slept, then I could talk to him, without an audience.

Issa released me from his gaze, probably just as disinterested as I was in the acting out of a romantic reunion. Sensing my discomfort, everyone else cut me some slack and prepared for takeoff.

The countryside dwarfed beneath us and the massive Atlantic Ocean dominated the view once again. The darkness outside my window was immense, but enveloped me with that same sense of comfort that I had described to Issa. We were no longer flying into an unknown fate or headed for a blazing inferno of danger. The fires of chaos had been extinguished, and the moon glistened from beyond with a cool glow. This time we sat quietly, gratefully, not anticipating much of anything but rest.

22

"I get my head bandage taken off today."

Musa stood in my doorway looking like a kid who was about to have a leg cast removed and play until he dropped.

"Wanna come with me?"

"No!" I laughed.

He smiled. "Come on! You can tell me if my head is still shaped right. I might be too afraid to look."

"It's only been three days. You're still gonna have to wear something over that cut."

"Yeah, but it won't be this big ass, mummy wrap."

"Ha! Thank God for that!"

He lightly patted the area where his head had been injured.

"You didn't hit the ground *that* hard." I joked.

"Thank goodness, right? You know," he lifted his good arm to lean against the wall, and stepped closer to me.

"getting shot really wasn't all that bad. It was just like, bang, and I was out."

"Wow. Really?"

"Yeah, well, you know I never saw it coming, so there was no fear or anticipation or anything."

"Oh. I get it."

"Must have been pretty hard for you guys to see, though."

"The worst!"

"But I heard you held it together and did what you had to do back there."

"Yeah well, it's not every day a girl gets nearly fed to hyenas and comes out unscathed."

"I hear ya… So, I was thinking, while we have a while to just relax… we should spend some time together. Never expected that we would end up chillin' in an African paradise when we were back in Philly getting chased by goons, but while we're here we should have some fun. Since we've gotten here, you and I just keep kinda passing by each other."

He waved his free hand back and forth in front of me to demonstrate the manner in which we "passed" each other.

"Hmm. Well, I didn't want to interfere with your time with your brothers."

"Um hmm." He nodded but he looked puzzled.

"And so much has happened, it's taken the last few days just for me to start processing the shock of everything. The quiet has been good for me, really."

"Oh, okay."

"A-and with everything that you've experienced, you know, physically— I just didn't think it was an appropriate time to, you know, do… whatever we were doing before."

While I rambled he looked at his hands then at me, then at his feet, then at me, then he patted his thighs as if checking their sturdiness and looked back at me. The whole time, he appeared confused.

"Jane," he finally said. "I was shot in the shoulder."

"I know that."

"Everything else works fine."

My face must have shown him that I was dumbfounded, but his expression indicated that there was no reason for me to expect anything different out of him.

"Whoa." I exclaimed. "Such an enthusiastic proposition right after we were all nearly ushered into the gates of hell is a bit much, even coming from you. Why don't you let *that* head heal before you start letting the other one take over."

He leaned his head back in amusement but the pain in his shoulder wouldn't let him break into a full-blown crack up.

"Besides," I said while leaning in to give his arm a comforting rub, "Our little encounter on the beach was not even a week ago. Too much too soon and there will be nothing left to discover, ya know? I bore easily."

Truth be told, I wasn't in a hurry to be intimate with Musa again, and it wasn't because I didn't enjoy our encounter. It had actually been fantastic. But the stress of the situation that we'd all just overcome was still making its exit from my system.

The fact that he was Issa's brother was nagging at me a little, too, even though I knew that I hadn't caused any rift between them. I didn't see any reason to rush with him and pile on more thoughts and emotions that I would need to process.

"Careful. Aren't you maimed, Frankenstein? You should still be dizzy." Issa walked toward us with his hands in his pockets and wearing a tepid grin.

"This guy!" Musa remarked.

Unaffected, Issa looked straight at his brother and said, "Jane, I'd like to speak with you for a moment, in private. Then you may continue as you wish." Slowly, he turned and looked at me.

"Oh, thanks for the permission." I answered giving no indication that I'd already decided to keep my conversation with Musa short.

Issa insisted. "Jane, I promise you both that I will only need a few moments of your time, and then you can be on your way."

"Ooo-kay." Musa stood straight up and gave in. "Let the man say his piece. I'll be in the hot tub."

As Musa strode back down the hall, Issa stepped in front of me to open the door. "After you."

"Thanks." I said. "So, what's up."

He sat down on a club chair and politely stretched out his hand toward my bed, gesturing for me to have a seat.

"Back in Harper," he began, "well, actually just after, on the MV Caterina, I had a lot of things on my mind."

"We all did."

"I know, but it wasn't just all that stuff— those thugs after us, preparing to take people's lives, the baby and Fatou, the money... I was thinking of the two of us."

The way he said *"the two of us"* in a lower pitch than the rest of his words and with a touch of seriousness mixed with tenderness and with his eyes peering straight into mine, made me feel a little awkward.

"The *two of us*." I said hoping for some clarification. I hoped he didn't think more of *"the two of us"* than I did. I thought I was off the hook, already.

"Yes," he went on, "the two of us. It was comforting having you there, helping me stay focused, keeping me from throwing up all over that little cabin on the boat. You helped me out a lot. If you hadn't been here... things could've gone another way. Everything could have gone another way."

I paused and looked down at the floor in order to let his genuine appreciation sink in.

"I'm a firm believer that all things happen for a reason." I said. "Must have been meant to be. I'm grateful that we're all okay."

He nodded in agreement and continued, "Normally, during this season of Ramadan, one might ask forgiveness for their wrongdoing as a part of the cleansing process. But with all that's happened, I just don't feel that would be enough. You asked me a question there, on that boat."

"I did?"

"Yeah. It was about you being my hitman."

"Ha! Oh. Turns out my services weren't needed after all, huh— not with Rambo and Black Diamond on our team."

He chuckled and shook his head. "You can enjoy a clear conscience."

"Almost." I nodded in amusement.

"But I thought about what you said, and I think I do owe you *something*."

"Issa, really, you don't owe me anything. We're young. We're both finding our way. I don't blame you for anything. I just hope for the best for you... And I hope you're not taking what's happened between Musa and I as me trying to be petty, or get some kind of twisted revenge or something. It's totally not that."

"That's not what I mean. And I know, I can tell that thing between you and Musa isn't revenge."

He understood, despite the rolling of his eyes. Thank goodness. I didn't want to clarify it for him by reminding him how tall, handsome, and charming Musa was, or how we were like two dolphins billowing blissfully in and out of the water that night back in Harper, or how his scent was enough to make me want to jump up and cling to his chest like an octopus– but I would if I had to.

He continued. "I could have cost you your life in the worst way, and I prevented you from moving on in a way that could have kept you safe. I've held you up here and jeopardized your reputation in your new job. That's not acceptable."

"Issa, don't do this. You didn't volunteer for this any more than I did. Truth is, I don't expect anything from you. Not anymore."

"Just let me finish. I wouldn't feel right knowing that I affected you like this and didn't try to make some of it right. Give me time to straighten some things out. After you get back home, there will be something there for you."

What could he be referring to? I wasn't planning on looking a gift horse in the mouth if he wanted to send me some small "thank you" gift, but I had truly been grateful for all the good that had transpired between us. Overcoming the threat of gruesome death put everything in perspective for me and made both our past dishonesty and immaturity seem like minor issues.

The man was alive with his dear family members, and expecting a baby. I had, once again, landed on my feet in spite of overwhelming odds. We were enjoying an unexpected vacation on the beautiful West African coast, and we all still had bright futures ahead. I didn't feel like I could ask for a better ending.

"Well, whatever this token of your appreciation is, I'm grateful for the thought. But most importantly, I'm thankful for you knocking off that hyena back in Frederick Douglas's bedroom!"

Wearing a satisfied smile, he stood to leave then said one last thing.

"Once, I heard some guy say that relationships are like flowers— if you don't water them they die."

"Flowers die whether you water them or not, Issa— fast. Some things are supposed to have short life spans."

I could see the sincerest appreciation in his eyes. We both gave each other an amiable glance, and he quietly let himself out of the room.

No more than ten seconds later, Musa was back and knocking on my door.

"So what's up? We chillin?"

"I cannot buh-lieve that you are right back here talking that same stuff… "

He just stood there grinning while I shook my head in amazement. We had a little staring contest. I was playful, but unrelenting. Finally, he blinked and dropped his head, still smirking.

"Where's the nearest beach?" I asked him.

"Oh shit!" he said, excited.

"Easy. I'm wearing a bathing suit this time. And Fatou told me the Cachupa that Jajah's cook makes is amazing. I am starving."

I can't swim like this." He said, trailing down the hall behind me.

"So we'll find some cool spot under a tree and have a beer. Chill out and heal!"

23

"Shouldn't we be wearing wet suits or something?" I asked Fatou.

"Nah!" she answered. "A wet suit for what? It's hot as hell out here."

"People wear them for protection." I argued.

"Come on!"

"What if this leash thing yanks on my leg and breaks it or something when I fall into a wave?"

"Jane, stop worrying. Surfing is about going with the flow of the waves and letting go. Relax! It's very fluid." She did a slow, loosey goosey dance with her hips and arms as if she was already immersed in the sea. She seemed a lot more relaxed and expressive lately, like a weight had been lifted, and she was more comfortable in her skin.

"When the heck did you learn to surf, anyway, between being a child soldier, running for your life, and escaping to the U.S.? That's some story you'll have for that baby."

She bent down to help me strap the surfboard leash to my leg. I ran my fingers up and down the board, across splotches of worn paint and faded lettering. I took comfort in the fact that its dominant color was my favorite royal blue.

"Well," she said, "I learned as a kid. You'll be surprised how many children in coastal African towns have taken to it. I haven't done it since then, though. It means a lot for me to be back in the water now."

She squinted with her hand over her brow to block the sun and looked longingly at the water. I hesitated to bring up more of the past, but I got the sense that mentioning the significance of this reunion with the sea was her way of welcoming the conversation.

"Issa told me that you moved to the States when you were sixteen. Was that right after everything happened with Frederick?"

We both waded slowly into the water as she surveyed the waves. After gently passing her hands through the water she said,

"It was only a few months before I got rescued, but it felt like forever. I don't know what was worse, the abuse or the requirement to fight and kill. I was always so scared that if I stayed in the army much longer, I would be too attached to the identity of a soldier to let it go. That's what happened to so many of those kids.

"That generation of child soldiers that's coming of age now, what are they doing? On the one hand it was hell. On the other, fighting was the only thing that gave them a sense of power and purpose. And the girls who fought—

they're shunned even more than the boys. No one will marry them. A lot of them are prostitutes, 'cause that's the only way to get by. They can't get jobs. They aren't seen as women because they fought. When they show child soldiers on the news or in movies, it's never the girls. We are invisible."

We jumped one last wave before Fatou decided we were finally far enough into the ocean to begin my first lesson. She demonstrated by lying down flat on her belly on the board and instructed me to do the same.

"Don't look at me like that. I'm not even showing."

"Okay, I know." I said with some skepticism. "What is it, like, the size of a peanut right now?"

"Something like that."

"The water doesn't make you nauseous?"

"Not at all! Stop acting like I'm fragile, girl. I'm the original mama. Anyway, if this is the last surf I get for a while, I'm definitely taking advantage of the chance."

I tried a couple of times to balance myself while lying flat on the board as she stood by.

"I don't know," she went on, "sometimes I think I should just accept the safer options in life and be thankful I didn't end up like so many of those other kids."

"And forfeit the chance to live your own life without anyone else deciding who you should be? No way!" I responded. "That's not the point. You have a chance at freedom, and it's your responsibility to take it."

"Jajah told me that he and some of his colleagues may have found my mom in Senegal. They were looking for a while but ramped up their efforts when we came here. They finally tried reaching a woman in Dakar and got a call back yesterday. If it's true... I think I'll stay there, at least for a while."

"That is amazing! I so wish you the best! I hope it all turns out perfectly—I know it will!"

I gave her a hug and realized that she was shaking. She was breathing a little heavy and had a stunned but hopeful look on her face.

"I was sure that those soldiers had killed everybody. I never heard from anyone once I moved to the U.S., and Issa and the boys, they were my only family then, I thought. After I escaped, they raided our neighborhood, and I knew they targeted my home. I hope I'm not disappointed, but I have a good feeling about this."

"I'm looking forward to the best for you." I said. "Now go take a rest! I think you've had enough for a minute."

I rolled my eyes as Issa and Jelaney waded into the water. I had hoped that Fatou would be the only person witnessing my clumsy attempt at surfing up close.

"If you stay out here too long tanning you'll have to come up with some other excuse for missing work." Issa said.

"Huh?"

"You go back there looking like you just took a vacation in the Caribbean and they'll know."

I barely dodged another wave and finally got a firm footing after struggling to free a lone grain of sand from my eyelid.

"Know what, Issa?"

He looked at Jelaney. They both chuckled as if they were already in on a very good joke.

"That toasty, bronze glow doesn't give you the convincing look of a sick person." Jelaney said.

"I don't want to think about that bank right now, Issa. Will you tell me what the heck you mean so I can get back to my surfing? What did you say when you called two weeks ago to tell them we'd be absent?"

Issa gave Jelaney another mischievous look.

"I told them that I caught some god awful, airborne, African disease from my visiting cousins, that you got it from me, and that we've been quarantined."

Would they actually fall for that? I worked for a bunch of attorneys who could sniff out a lie like drug dogs. And who knows the kinds of crazy stares and treatment I'd get returning to work after catching some *"god awful, African disease"*!

"You didn't!"

He smiled and nodded his head.

"Quarantine?" I asked, baffled.

"It's no problem! Salim has a few friends at the CDC in Atlanta. We have doctor's notes or whatever the hell they'll need to see. They bought it. They wished us a speedy recovery. You'll probably have a mailbox full of get well gifts when you get back home."

"What did you tell them we caught?"

To this question, Jelaney responded with a spurt of giggling which could simply not be contained. He gave me a sympathetic glance, but lowered his head in hearty laughter nonetheless.

"Dengue fever." Issa said.

"You've gotta be kidding me." I said, unable to ignore the beautiful coincidence. "Dengue is a mosquito-borne disease."

"Eh, whatever! We got over it."

24

The night before our flight back home I nearly fell asleep in the bathroom. I must have been in there for at least an hour basking in the serenity of its flawless white tile interior and its deep, luxurious bathtub. After Jajah noticed how quiet I was at dinner, he asked a house girl to draw me a bubble bath with daisies and a dash of calming essential oils.

I couldn't help but be burdened with concerns. I'd been given a new lease on life, but what would I be doing with it? What opportunities would I have to look forward to back home? How long would it take me to get back on my feet again? How could I be happy in the meantime on my way to the life that I really wanted— a life that I had already worked so hard to establish, to no avail?

Though my life had been spared, so many of the things that I once held dear had died off or were taking their last labored breaths: my dreams, my spiritual beliefs, and my notions of who I was. My original perceptions of life and what it should have been were fading.

I had spent years in what seemed like a constant state of alarm— desperate to get away and build my own life; desperate for the student loans to be approved so I could stay in school one more semester and hopefully graduate; desperate to keep my grades up, my car on the road and my bills paid; desperate to find decent work and to juggle it all successfully. There always seemed to be some crisis to overcome.

Then, the things that I feared most happened and rendered all my desperation pointless. Now, infinite possibilities filled the voids. I had a sense of renewed adventure to accompany my sense of loss.

I sat thinking about the events that had happened since I head butted Issa in the nose and vowed to myself that I'd never speak to him again. Instead, like it or not, he'd become something like my blood brother.

As I drifted into that mysterious space between sleep and lucidity, I sensed a presence nearby. I chose to listen carefully rather than immediately jerk myself awake again, like I usually did in the presence of some unknown nightly visitor. Having faced the mystique of death one more time, I was more ready than ever to accept a greeting from across the divide. Maybe whoever it was carried just the message I needed.

I heard something small, like an ink pen or pencil, fall to the floor in the next room.

"Okay, that was real." I said to myself.

I immediately opened my eyes and stayed still, scanning the room for something that could be used as a weapon. There was a small vase on the floor just a few feet away, but if I moved right then, the sound of me sloshing out of the tub could be heard by whoever was in my room.

I waited to see if the intruder would leave. There were footsteps getting closer and closer to my bathroom.

I stared at the blanket of bubbles in my tub, wondering if I could effectively hide myself under it and hold my breath for however long it would take to stay out of sight. Then, the door slowly began to open.

He could immediately see that I was startled by his presence.

"I'm sorry. Didn't mean to scare you." Issa said.

He brought one hand forward from behind his back, revealing some Pontche de Coco which had been served inside a halved coconut shell.

"This has been significantly spiked," I said after inspecting it playfully with a sniff, "presumably with rum."

He nodded graciously.

"You better be glad I couldn't reach that vase. You could have lost your head."

He took a seat on the edge of the tub and relished my enjoyment of the drink as much as I did the sweet coconut flavor and its spicy kick.

"I think I already did." he said. Then he leaned in close to me, lifted my chin and gently touched my forehead with his lips. It was the first time he kissed me.

25

I sat on the edge of my courthouse seat on pins and needles. Could I really pull this off? Did I have my head on straight after getting back from the disaster in Monrovia?

I wasn't sure, but it didn't matter. I had been in a huge rush because the Sheriff's sale for the house on Pelham Road had been scheduled just days from my arrival back home. I hadn't had any time to do all the due diligence, but there was no way I'd miss this opportunity.

Before our burgeoning relationship took a sharp turn for the worse, Jack, as my career mentor, had taught me that there was a protocol for buying distressed properties like this one. He would have advised me to go to a few auctions first to get a feel for the auctioneer's reaction time and figure out where the best seats are. He would have told me to visit the property again to inspect the exterior, visit the Office of Licensing and Inspections to see if there were any violations or zoning issues, talk to the neighbors to get the low down on the owner's habits and weaknesses. I hadn't had time for any of that.

Issa had been exactly right— when I got back home, my P.O. box was full of cards and notices for packages that I'd need to pick up. It was like Christmas, an outpouring of genuine compassion from the folks at the bank. There was also a card from Issa in which he expressed his gratitude for all that we'd overcome. True to form, he kept his very sincere sentiments short and to the point:

"Now that you're back home safe and sound, it's best you get settled in as soon as possible. I hope this helps. I guess it makes us even."

I opened the envelope and took a closer look inside to find the notification for a bank wire transfer that he had sent on my behalf. Then I literally had to call for front desk assistance to my hotel room, because upon realizing that the wire transfer was in the amount of $100,000 I almost passed out, ran across the room for my cell phone in order to call *somebody* to share the news, got paranoid all of a sudden and decided to stop and think carefully about telling anyone, made a sharp pivot on my foot, fell and hurt my ankle, then laid on the floor laughing in agony for the next five minutes.

I finally got up and scrambled around the room in my underwear, tears streaming down my face, trying to hide the notification so hotel staff wouldn't see it if I couldn't eventually pull myself together and someone showed up to help me. It was a crazy scene, but I eventually had a glass of wine, said a prayer and calmed down.

I didn't have to think twice about what I'd do with the money. First, buy the house and sock away a reserve for taxes then pay off a good chunk of my student loan debt. And, since I couldn't actually live in the house yet, I'd get another apartment, pay rent a year in advance, and figure out the rest later.

From the second row of the court room, I braced myself for the bidding as officers rattled off a bunch of instructions: Bid within your means. Pay off your purchase in thirty days. Lowest possible bid is $800, increases by $100 increments until $20,000 is reached, then increases in $500 increments until $50,000 is reached...Blah, blah, blah. Yeah, yeah, yeah. *Just get on with it!*

The house on Pelham road was the first house on the list, and I didn't hesitate to pounce with an opening bid as soon as the officer announced the address.

I instinctively clutched my purse with my left hand as it rested under my right arm. I envisioned handing over the collection of cashier's checks that I had made out in different denominations in case the final price didn't quite match my estimate.

The home's market value had plummeted to $55,000 and I didn't want to pay more than sixty percent of that which would be $33,000. To offset the insanity of this decision, I would at least remain disciplined about my spending limit. My small stack of checks totaled no more than the twenty percent required for down payment, so $6600 would have to get the job done.

I forced my back into the chair as the officer read the property description so that I wouldn't actually be sitting on the edge of my seat with anticipation. Didn't want to appear nervous.

I overheard someone chatting about the house and the man who had been living there.

"Ya, know I think he's still in that house. Whoever gets it may have a real time trying to get him outta there."

It was a minor hiccup, in my opinion. I would not be deterred.

"...We're gonna start the bidding..." the officer said.

My hand flew up in a flash.

I and three other investors around the room placed rapid bids until the price reached $15,000. By the time it reached $25,000 there were only two of us left. I jumped on it.

The sheriff raised the bid again.

"$25,500," said a clear masculine voice in the back of the room." I recognized the guy as someone Jack had once introduced me to on a property visit. He'd been an investor for a while, purchasing smaller rowhomes and duplexes in Germantown, so this type of property didn't match the others in his holdings, as far as I knew. Maybe this was experimental or a whim and his motivation was only lukewarm.

I grabbed the next bid without hesitation. The bidding bounced between us until the price reached $29,000.

He gave me a quick look but kept the expression of his uncertainty in check.

Once the price reached $31,000, he had had enough.

"$31,500. Anyone? Do we have more bids?" the officer asked.

"$31,500." I said, ready for more— but not much more.

There was silence.

I folded my arms, sat back in my chair with a tremble, and exhaled with satisfaction.

"Sold."

From The Author

Joy Outlaw
www.inanna-joy.com

    I'm an inspirational author who uses snippets from my journey of life and love—my questions, problems, screw-ups, and victories, and those of the people around me—to fuel self-discovery. I'm a curious observer and determined seeker, sharing my lessons and not-so-humble opinions with anyone who'll delight in pondering with me.

    Georgia-born and Virginia-bred, I'm currently making a life in the mid-atlantic U.S. region with two fascinating tweens who call me "mom". I'm a writer for hire with a slew of creative endeavors and career attempts in my wake. Somewhere along the way, I picked up some descriptors: Mystic Muse, Scribbling Sphinx, Wondering Woman, Nightshift Novelist... Theevolution is real and it continues daily.

    Words are my stock and trade and the primary medium with which I paint my destiny. I believe that everything begins with them. They are the spells we use to destroy and create. I enjoy creating most, and I intend to make some pretty good shit. So strap in. It'll be a bumpy ride, and it'll only get better.

Wait! Don't leave yet.

We've only just begun.

Thanks for reading Things Fall Together. If you haven't yet checked out

Pretty Little Mess,

also in the Jane Luck Adventures series, what are you waiting for? You can read that while the next series installment is in the works, and when you visit

amazon.com/author/joyoutlaw,

please leave a review. Your thoughts in the conversation will invite others to discover this dynamic series and the alluring author behind this and many other captivating stories.

Share your thoughts now and stay tuned for more!

Made in the USA
Middletown, DE
18 July 2022

69565910R00168